EAT BUGS

〰〰〰 **PITCH** 〰〰〰

PARTNERS

EAT BUGS
PITCH
PARTNERS

Prospect Heights Public Library
12 N. Elm Street
Prospect Heights, IL 60070
www.phpl.info

BY HEATHER ALEXANDER
WITH LAURA D'ASARO AND ROSE WANG, THE FOUNDERS OF *CHIRPS™*
ILLUSTRATED BY VANESSA FLORES

FOR DIANA, MY FOREVER FRIEND, ALWAYS ONLY A PHONE CALL AWAY—HA

TO ALL THE PEOPLE WHO CARRIED US ALONG THE WAY: MERYL,
LIZ, MAX, MEGHAN, JENNA, GREG, BOB, TAMMY, LUIS, I-LAB TEAM,
PHILIPPE, MARK, CLAY, JOHN, STEVE, JAMES, PAUL, ZAC, SCOTT,
ANGIE, ECHOING GREEN FAMILY, CHICAGO IDEAS WEEK FOLKS,
AND ALL OUR FRIENDS AND FAMILY WHO HELPED US BAKE 10,000
CRICKET COOKIES IN TWO WEEKS, PACK THOUSANDS OF BAGS
OF CHIPS, AND ATE BUGS BEFORE ANYONE ELSE DARED—LD + RW

FOR MAMI AND PAPI, BECAUSE YOU NEVER
STOPPED BELIEVING IN MY BIG DREAM—VF

PENGUIN WORKSHOP
An Imprint of Penguin Random House LLC, New York

Text copyright ©2021 by Heather Alexander LLC, Laura D'Asaro, and Wei Wang.
Illustrations copyright © 2021 by Vanessa Flores. All rights reserved.
Published by Penguin Workshop, an imprint of Penguin Random House LLC, New York. PENGUIN
and PENGUIN WORKSHOP are trademarks of Penguin Books Ltd, and the W colophon is
a registered trademark of Penguin Random House LLC. Manufactured in China.

If you want to experiment with eating insects, please don't eat insects you catch in the wild.
You can purchase edible insects that are farmed and have gone through quality testing.
Also, if you are allergic to crustaceans or shellfish, you may also be sensitive to insects.

Visit us online at www.penguinrandomhouse.com.

Library of Congress Cataloging-in-Publication Data is available upon request.

ISBN 9780593096192   10 9 8 7 6 5 4 3 2 1

PROLOGUE
HALLIE

Here's the secret to building a business: Be like the spiders. Not just any spiders—the spiders of the South American rainforest.

The spider is a solitary creature. It spins its own web. Captures its own food. Eats solo. Check out any spider in your yard or corner of a ceiling. A loner, right?

But not the *Anelosimus eximius*. Yesterday in science class, we watched a video about them. These spiders aren't like other spiders. They're "social spiders." They live together in massive colonies. Fifty thousand spiders crawling together! Think of all those legs! These social spiders figured out that if they spin a gigantic web together, they catch more prey than going it alone. Heavy rain—which happens constantly since, hello, it's the rainforest—can majorly wreck a web. But the spiders learned it's way easier to repair the damage with thousands of legs instead of just eight.

I wish we'd known about the rainforest spiders before everything happened.

You see, Jaye and I were a team. We had each other. We had a plan.

But, it turns out, what we really needed was a whole mess of spiders.

A much bigger web.

And an *enormous* platter of nachos.

CHAPTER 1
JAYE

"I love the chip aisle." I grabbed Hallie's hand and pulled her with me. We giggled, tripping and skidding around a mother pushing her chubby toddler in a shopping cart.

"I do, too," Hallie agreed. "Obviously."

"No, even before we started this, the chip aisle was my place." My eyes scanned the colorful, shiny bags standing at attention on the shelves. "If Nai Nai's in a good mood, she lets me pick a bag. Choosing is serious business."

I glanced over my shoulder and spotted my

grandmother in her olive-green quilted coat. She was waiting in line at the seafood counter. Nai Nai always insisted our fish be weighed at least twice to make sure the scale was correct, so I had plenty of time.

Hallie smacked her lips loudly. The mother with the cart stopped and looked our way.

"What're you doing?" I whispered. Hallie wasn't like me. She didn't care if people stared at her. In fact, I think she kind of liked it.

"I'm seeing what kind of chip mood I'm in." Hallie made more loud smacking sounds. "It's like a taste test, but without the food. You *pretend* you're eating." She stood on her tiptoes, reaching for the kettle corn. "I'm thinking sweet."

"Spicy and hot for me. Always." I pointed to an orange bag on a bottom shelf.

"Check out the wacky flavors." Hallie's long chestnut hair bounced as she spread her arms wide. "I mean, dill pickle tortilla chips? Really? We can make up such better flavors. What about cheddar caramel potato chips?"

"Or pineapple chili chips?" I suggested.

"Cheesy tomato?" Hallie offered. "Garlic butter banana?"

"How about hot-and-sour soup chips?"

Hallie and I tossed ideas back and forth at lightning speed. We were good at doing that.

"Icy cucumber lime."

"Honey vanilla peanut butter."

"Red-fire cinnamon spice!"

Suddenly I got worried. "Hold up. Are our chips okay? Should we be adding more flavors?"

"No way. Our recipe rocks," Hallie told me. "Besides, Mr. T said to keep it simple while we build the company."

Mr. T is Mr. Thompson, our teacher for Business Education and Entrepreneurship. That's the sixth-grade elective class we both chose at Brookdale Middle School.

Our class project last month was to create our own startup business. Mr. Thompson picked our partners. He paired me with Hallie Amberose.

I'm not going to lie. I was *not* happy.

Hallie wasn't one of the popular kids. Not even a tiny bit. And I was.

Well, I was friends with Spencer Montan and Erica Sanchez, which is kind of the same thing.

Then Hallie volunteered to eat a cricket on our class field trip to the zoo. After that, Spencer and Erica called her "Bug Girl." But Hallie didn't care. In fact, she decided our startup company should sell chips made from edible bugs. Crushed crickets, actually.

Making bug chips with Bug Girl? I was *doubly* not happy.

But that was back in September. It's November now, and a lot has changed.

Hallie and I have become friends. She's way nicer and

more fun than Erica and Spencer. And I'm really trying not to care (as much) about being popular. But part of me still cares (a little).

And I think our cricket chips are PURE GENIUS.

Delicious, too.

I'm all about edible bugs now.

"Ta-da!" Hallie unzipped her purple backpack and pulled out a plastic baggie. The red-and-white homemade label on the front read:

CHIRPS CHIPS

The world's first cricket chip

Pushing aside the bags of pretzels, she placed it in the center of the middle shelf.

We stepped back to admire it. This was the dream. Our cricket chips on store shelves around the world!

"Chirps belongs right there," Hallie said confidently.

"I don't know." I couldn't keep the doubt from my voice. "It's a long way from my kitchen to Wegmans. I mean, let's get real. Hot Cheetos aren't made in a house in upstate New York by two twelve-year-olds."

"We're just starting out, Jaye. You've got to *bee-lieve*." Hallie dragged out the word *believe*.

"I believe in our chips." They're made with cricket powder, so they're super healthy for people and the planet. Everyone who's tried them agrees they taste better—and a bit nuttier—than regular chips. "But it took us almost six weeks to get the recipe right. And we only came in *second* in the school pitch competition—"

"Second is good," Hallie cut in.

"We didn't win," I pointed out.

"So what? The top two teams still move on to the county pitch competition. We get another chance to win." Hallie grinned. Her smile had a way of overtaking her entire face.

I wrapped a long strand of my black hair around my

finger. I stared at our little baggie on the shelf, dwarfed by the big, well-known brands. "We have no money, Hals. How can we possibly turn our chips into a snack sensation with no money?"

"We can make money. Maybe I can walk dogs. There are lots of dogs in my neighborhood. And you can babysit—"

"I hate babysitting," I reminded her. Watching my seven-year-old brother, Eddie, was bad enough.

"Okay, fine. I know, we'll collect our old toys and have a yard sale. We can sell our baby stuff, too. Like blankets and rattles." Hallie never ran out of ideas.

I twisted my hair tighter. "I don't really have any."

I'd moved here from China when I was in kindergarten. My baby stuff had been left behind. Or given away, I guess. And Eddie still played with most of my old toys. I didn't have anything to sell to make the kind of money we needed.

Hallie planted her hands on her hips. "We'll figure it out. We'll find a way."

"You think?"

"Yes! This is too important. Our chips are filled with protein, and eating crickets instead of a hamburgers helps with climate change, because cows use so much water and grass and . . ." Hallie was throwing out the facts I already knew. "We *have* to do this. You and me. I promise you, Jaye. Someday our chips will be on every supermarket shelf in the nation!"

I grinned. "Not the nation. The world! Come on, Hals, you've got to *bee-lieve!*"

Hallie raised her two pointer fingers to her head and wiggled them like antennae.

I did the same. This was our special never-give-up cricket signal.

"Hey, want to try some chips?" Hallie called to a bearded guy in a baseball cap who was reaching for pretzels. She pointed to our tiny bag. "They're going to be the next big thing."

"Bigger than big!" I cried.

"Huge!" Hallie added. "Ginormous!"

The bearded guy shot us a confused look.

Hallie didn't care. She grabbed both of my hands. Together we spun in a circle right in the middle of the snack aisle. Neither of us could stop laughing.

Excitement tingled from my fingers to my toes. This wasn't just a school project anymore. Or even a corner lemonade stand. We were going to build a *real* business. I'd never been at the center of something so important.

And Hallie made me believe.

In us.

CHAPTER 2
HALLIE

  Chip Domination Road Map

1. ~~Win school pitch~~

2. Win county pitch

3. Win state pitch

4. Win national pitch

5. Be the BIGGEST, BEST food company EVER and get the WHOLE WORLD to eat bugs!

"Jaye Wu and Hallie Amberose?" The woman at the sign-up desk handed us a shiny blue folder. *PITCH! The Ultimate Kid-preneurship Pitch Competition* was emblazoned in yellow across the front.

"That's us." My voice echoed off Hotel Tremain's high ceiling. Mom had dropped us off at the historic redbrick hotel in the center of Andersville. Then she went to the Saturday afternoon farmer's market.

I gazed around the fancy ballroom. Round wooden tables had been pushed to the sides, and rows of padded maroon leather chairs filled the center. Kids waited in clumps for the information session to start. I spotted Raul Cortez and Peter Rank. Their Summer Sled had won first place in our school pitch competition. It's a board that gets attached to huge blocks of ice, made from molds. You can carry the ice in a cooler to a park, and the Summer Sled lets you sled down a grassy hill. No snow needed! A total game changer for kids in warm-weather places.

"There's Bryar Besson." Jaye pointed to a girl in a green dress with a long thick ponytail.

"Who's that?" I glanced down at my T-shirt and rainbow-striped leggings. Should I've dressed up for this?

"Bryar plays on my soccer team. I didn't know her school did this, too." Jaye walked into the ballroom, and I followed. "And what's Li-Ming Zhao doing here? I just saw him at Chinese school this morning."

"I guess he won his school competition, too." Many middle schools in Kirra County had hosted an entrepreneur competition. Pitch! was like *Shark Tank* but for kids. The top two teams at each school had come to this special meeting today to learn the rules for the next competition.

I watched Jaye wave to other kids. Jaye's always in the middle of a big group. Her grandma drives her all over to soccer practice, cello lessons, orchestra rehearsal, Chinese school, and I don't know what else with lots of different kids. I knew no one there. But that's probably because I go home every day right after school.

And because I'm not a group-friend person. Never have been.

"Jaye!" A tiny girl hurried over. She wore sweatpants and a hot-pink leotard, as if she'd come straight from gymnastics.

"Hey, Posie!" Jaye turned to me. "We went to Federal together. Until she moved."

Federal was Jaye's elementary school. I'd gone to Lynwood, on the other side of town.

"Where's Spencer?" Posie looked past me.

"He's not here," Jaye said.

"Oh? I figured he'd be your partner." Posie seemed confused. "I mean, you guys do everything together."

"Yeah, well, not anymore . . ." Jaye twirled her hair. She does that when she's uncomfortable.

"What happened?" Posie gasped. "Did you have a fight?"

"Nothing like that." I stepped forward to rescue Jaye. "*I'm* her partner."

Spencer lived across the street from Jaye, and they'd been best friends since kindergarten. The kids in our grade think he's the coolest. But they're wrong—he's horribly mean. Spencer stole the first business idea Jaye came up with and lied about it, then their friendship crashed and burned. But things weren't so great between them even before he did that.

Now Jaye was friends with me.

Sometimes I get scared she'll go back to Spencer and Erica Sanchez and all those other popular kids. That she won't think I'm cool enough. She told me she never would, but . . .

"EAT BUGS." Posie read aloud the words on my black T-shirt. "What's that?"

"It's our mission statement." I'd ironed the white felt letters onto my black T-shirt this morning. I'd made a matching shirt for Jaye, but she'd put her navy sweater over it. "Our tortilla chips are super healthy and yummy, because they're made with cricket powder. They have three times more protein than regular potato chips. Did you know crickets use way less water and natural resources than cows? So food made from crickets is way better for the planet—"

Jaye touched my arm. "Too much info, Hals."

When I'm excited, I rev up and can't stop talking.

"What're you doing?" Jaye asked Posie.

"My company delivers personalized activity kits to kids in hospitals." Posie explained how each kid answered an online questionnaire, and then their kit came with books and games chosen especially for them, and even a hospital gown in their favorite color.

Two boys from her school came over and told us about the app they designed. It let animal shelters post short videos with great graphics. This helped get even the most scraggly pups adopted.

"Welcome, innovators and entrepreneurs!" A bald man

in a dark suit tapped a microphone at a podium. "Everyone find a seat."

I headed to the first row, but Jaye grabbed my sleeve. "No way! Too close."

I followed her to the fourth row, next to Raul and Peter. I opened my Listbook to a fresh page. I love to make lists!

Sometimes they're serious, like *Important Books I Should Read* or *Murals to Paint on My Bedroom Wall* or *Birthday Gifts for Henry* (he's my big brother).

And lots of times they're just fun, like *Words that Rhyme with Clementine* or *The Top Five Cutest Baby Animals.*

The guy at the podium spoke again. "I'm Lewis Fletcher, and I'm a teacher at Mount Bancroft Middle." Two kids near the back let out a whoop. I turned to the teachers gathered at the side and waved to Mr. T. I wanted our teacher to have a fan section, too.

"You've all been hard at work. You've developed your own business, created a product, and you're figuring out how to sell and market it. You were chosen to move on to the county-wide competition. This next level will not be easy." Fletcher grew serious. "Look to your left. Now look to your right. This room is filled with extreme talent."

I twisted in my seat. Desire to win shone bright in every kid's eyes.

"The Kirra County Pitch Competition is on December fourth." As he gave details about where it was, I peeked at the calendar on my phone. Today was November 6. December 4 was in four weeks.

Plenty of time.

"Here's how it will work," he continued. "Each team will have two minutes to present their business plan. You must tell us why your company and product is important, the problem it is solving, and how you plan to grow the business. Then the judges will ask you some questions. All the judges own their own businesses, so be prepared, kids. They know what's up."

Jaye and I had already done this for our school competition. We'd just do the same thing again. Easy!

"The first-place winner will receive a cash prize of one thousand dollars. Second place will be five hundred dollars. The money must go back into your business."

That was mega money! I reached over and squeezed Jaye's hand. Our Pitch Partner Power Pulse, we called it.

"The first- and second-place winners will both move on to the *state* pitch competition held in New York City"—Mr. Fletcher paused for effect—"and they'll stay in a luxury hotel for the weekend."

The room erupted. This was huge! I'd never been to New York City.

Mr. Fletcher tapped the microphone to quiet us. Then he smiled mischievously. "But . . . there's a twist. A few *new* things you have to do."

I scribbled down everything he said.

1. show an INNOVATIVE way we made people aware of our product (like advertising or a big event or a viral video)

2. show how the $ works (cost to make it/price we sell it for/how we'll use $$$ WHEN we win)

3. complete a Special Challenge (????)

Before I could ask Jaye what she thought that meant, we were divided into groups.

"Foodies with me," a tall woman with sun-bleached hair called from the far corner of the room. The four food companies in the competition hurried over. Jaye's friend Bryar was there. The woman, whose name was Liz Rees, had us sit in a circle and introduce our products. There was a muffin company (that was Bryar's), a hot sauce company, a gourmet samosa company, and our cricket chips. Ms. Rees shared the story of starting her advertising agency,

CurrentZ, and told about her work with startups. Then she asked us to share the inspiration for our company names.

"Ours is obvious," I said, when she got to us. "A cricket chirps, and Chirps sounds like chips. And it's an alliteration."

I expected Ms. Rees to chuckle. I mean, it's a super-catchy name. But she just nodded, and went on to the next team. Finally, after a lot of instructions on how to give a sales pitch, Ms. Rees handed all four food companies the same neon yellow card with the Special Challenge written on it.

> Sell 200 units of your product.
> Keep track of each sale.
> No sales permitted to
> family members or relatives.

"Two hundred? That's a lot," Jaye whispered. So far we'd only sold five bags since the last competition. And three of them were to Jaye's grandma.

"I know, right?" said Bryar. "Our muffins are large, so people won't want to eat a bunch at once."

"No big deal," one of the hot sauce boys boasted. "We've got two hundred bottles in my garage. We'll sell them all this week. Like this." He snapped his fingers.

"Yeah? So will we," I quickly said.

"You'll never beat our hot sauce," the boy taunted. "It's on fire!"

"Oh, burn!" His partner fist-bumped him.

"Our chips will *crunch* the competition!" I exclaimed. Bryar laughed at my comeback.

"Good pun, right?" I asked Jaye. We liked to try to out-pun each other.

Jaye pulled me aside. She looked concerned. "We've only got a few bags of chips to sell."

"So we'll make some more." Sure, we had to step up our game, but I wasn't worried. We could bake and sell a bunch of chips.

Everyone filed into the lobby to find their parents. Ever since I can remember, I've been the last kid picked up from everything. My mom's an artist, and she's always getting lost in clouds of creative thought. At least, that's what she says. She shows up eventually, so I usually don't stress it. But today I felt embarrassed. Jaye wasn't used to waiting around. Her grandma was always first in line at school pickup.

I fumbled an apology, then asked if she wanted to sleep over tonight.

"I can't. Family dinner."

I chewed the inside of my cheek. She'd given the same excuse last week. Why didn't she ever want to sleep over?

Jaye sat on a blue velvet bench, her forehead wrinkled in thought. "Can I use your Listbook?"

I hesitated. My Listbook is like my journal, diary, and assignment pad rolled into one. I never let anyone write in it. Until now. I slowly handed it over.

She wrote furiously, her left hand cupped protectively

over her tiny notes. I sat next to her and waited silently.
Finally, she showed me.

▶▶▶ <u>What We Need to Make 200 Bags of Chips</u> ◀◀◀

- 3,000 crickets

- 8 pounds of corn masa

- LOTS of spices

- olive oil

- mixing bowl & spoon & rolling pin

- baking trays & spatula

- 200 small bags

- 200 labels

- KITCHEN!!!!

"A kitchen? What about your kitchen?" I cried.

We'd cooked our other batches of chips there. Nai Nai helped. Her grandma lives with them and takes care of Jaye and her brother, Eddie. Jaye's mom helped us once, which was great because she's a scientist, and she taught us how to precisely measure out all the ingredients. It turns out cooking is a lot like doing an experiment in a lab. But Jaye's mom is *always* working. Her dad, too. They're never around.

"Eddie has a big tennis tournament soon. He has all these lessons and a mini tournament leading up to it," Jaye explained. "Nai Nai has to take him to everything. We need to hit pause on cooking, because we can't use the oven without her."

Nai Nai rules over their spotless, organized kitchen.

"A pause? No way! We'll just cook at my house"—I caught Jaye rolling her eyes—"or not."

My kitchen was cramped and the counters were cluttered with stuff, like the blender Henry was taking apart, the tangled scarf my mom was knitting, and highlighter pens my dad leaves behind. It's not the best if you're making food to sell.

"And we need to buy ingredients. Where are we going to get all those bugs? Crickets cost a lot of money. And we have zero money," Jaye reminded me. "Except for the twenty dollars Auntie Lin sent for my birthday."

"That's something. I have ten dollars."

"It's not enough."

My phone beeped with a text. Mom was outside.

"We'll figure it out. Remember what Mr. T said in class? The greatest entrepreneurs aren't afraid to think outside the box." I grabbed Jaye's hand and gave it a squeeze. "So that's what we'll do."

CHAPTER 3
JAYE

"I'm bored," I told Nai Nai Tuesday afternoon.

"No, you are not." Behind her large black-framed glasses, her dark eyes tracked the flight of the ball on the court below. She clocked each missed shot and footwork fumble.

Eddie would be asked about them later. His tennis mattered in our family. A lot.

I watched through the tinted window separating us from the indoor court. He slammed the ball for a crosscourt winner. Everyone at the tennis center calls my skinny brother a "prodigy," which means he has mind-boggling talent.

I used to take tennis lessons, too. No one ever called me a prodigy. Most of my shots landed in the net. Coach Yi kept telling my parents I had bad eye-hand coordination. For the longest time, Baba refused to believe him. My dad was great at tennis when he was growing up in China. He wanted me to be great, too.

Then Baba saw Eddie play—and realized his talent had landed in his son. He let me stop tennis. He said it would give me time to focus on my other talents.

Except I don't have any other talents.

I play cello, but I've never made first chair in the orchestra. I play soccer, but I rarely score a goal. I sing in the school choir, but I've never gotten a solo. I get good grades, but Bhavik Patel gets better grades.

"I finished my homework." I pushed my Language Arts

questions toward Nai Nai. I spend so many afternoons at this wooden table doing homework while Eddie practices. "Can I get something from the vending machine?"

"No. You already ate." Nai Nai always packs our snacks. She says it's silly to pay when we have perfectly good food at home.

"But I'm hungry." I stood and shook out my legs.

"Jie, you are not hungry. You are bored." She spoke to me in Mandarin as she kept her eyes on Eddie.

"I already said *that*." I sighed, frustrated. My gaze wandered from the muted ESPN announcer on the TV in the corner to the fliers tacked on the bulletin board outside the pro shop. One caught my attention. I stepped closer.

Rec Center Renovation Complete!

New Classes, New Facilities!

Check Us Out! Grand Opening Celebration December 1.

"The rec center's ready. Can I take a look? Please?" Our town rec center was attached to the tennis center, so

I wouldn't be leaving the complex.

Nai Nai leaned forward and squinted to better see Coach Yi adjust Eddie's serve. "Ten minutes. Be back in ten minutes."

I hurried off before she could change her mind.

I pushed open the door between the tennis center and the rec center. The odor of fresh paint greeted me. My sneakers squeaked against the shiny linoleum floor as I made my way down the quiet hall, peeking into different rooms. A weight room, filled with new machines and shiny dumbbells. A room with mats and a ballet barre. A room with tiny chairs and toys.

"Hi there!" A woman with two loose, brown braids popped up from behind a low bookshelf, startling me. "Tell me, does this look like a parade to you?" She was arranging small paper bag puppets in a line.

"Yeah, I guess. I'm sorry," I said, suddenly unsure if I was allowed to be here. "I was just looking around."

"You don't need to be sorry, sweetie. We're not officially open, but we're setting up today. This is the childcare room, if you didn't already figure that out." She inhaled deeply. "Ah, Irv's testing the new ovens. Sourdough, I think."

I caught a whiff of toasty bread.

The woman grinned. "Let's go get a sample. But be warned: Irv can be grouchy, if you know what I mean."

I didn't. I hung back as she burst into the gleaming kitchen next door, all smiles and greetings.

"Deanna, I'm busy here." An older man hunched over a long granite counter. He jammed the keyboard of a laptop angrily with one finger. "Why doesn't this tab button work? And the spacing is all wrong." His bushy gray hair stuck out on the sides, and wire-rimmed glasses rested near the tip of his nose.

"Do you need help, Irv?" Deanna asked sweetly.

"No! Why would you say that?" His sounded annoyed. "I don't know why I agreed to this."

"Well, the bread smells delicious." Deanna pointed to two loaves cooling on the stovetop. One loaf was already sliced. "I bet it tastes delicious, too. Hint, hint."

Irv straightened and wiped his palms on his white apron. Then he handed her a piece of bread. "Go on with you. I got things to do."

"What about for my friend here?" Deanna nodded toward me. "This is—"

"Jaye," I stepped forward timidly.

Irv looked me over as I accepted the slice he'd placed on a paper towel. "You're young. You must know about computers. Better than Deanna here." He pointed to the screen. "Can you center that?"

It only took me a second to format his text block. It was a recipe for roasted chicken.

"What about a border?" he asked. "Can you do that?"

"Sure." I added a red border. "What's this for?"

"Stupid cookbook," he grumbled. "I volunteered to

teach the cooking classes here. That's all. But Bess—she's the rec center director and my daughter-in-law—has this fancy plan to give out a cookbook pamphlet thing at the grand opening party. She's making me type up and design my recipes. I'm a chef, not a book designer! That's just the first recipe. I have twenty-nine more to go."

I changed the border to blue, then green.

"Green looks nice." Irv sighed. "Milly would've known how to do this."

"Milly's his wife," Deanna whispered. "She passed at the beginning of the year."

"What's with the whispering? It's not a secret. I know Milly's dead!" Irv wasn't very nice to Deanna.

"Should I save this in a file for you?" I asked, suddenly eager to get back.

"Yes. How do you do that?" He leaned in.

I talked him through it slowly, step by step. I'd done this a lot with Nai Nai. The simplest things on the computer made her anxious. She's so afraid to mess up. She thinks the computer will explode or something. Irv was acting the same way.

"Do you cook?" Irv asked when we'd finished.

"Me? No. Well, actually, kind of. I just started to."

"Cookies, right? I bake those with my granddaughter, Mari." His pale blue eyes softened.

"Cricket chips."

"Say that again." He tilted his head as if he'd heard wrong.

I told him about Chirps. "Everyone likes chips, that's

why we chose to make them. The crickets get roasted in the oven, then crushed into powder that's used to make the chips. People like that better."

Irv shook his head in disbelief. "It's a bad idea. They'll never sell."

"I think they will." I explained our plan to make foods that don't harm the environment. Crickets are a more sustainable choice than meat. And as the world's population grows, bugs can feed millions more people. "Edible insects will become one of the most important food sources in the future. Plus, a quarter of the world already eats them."

"*Pssshhh.*" Irv waved me off. "Come to one of my cooking classes, and I'll show you food. Creamy pumpkin soup. Apple strudel. And in this swanky new setup."

For the first time, I took in the kitchen. Two big ovens. An eight-burner stove. A stainless steel refrigerator. Stacks of pots and baking trays.

"That won't work, Irv. Your classes are only in the

mornings while Jaye's probably in school," Deanna gently reminded him.

"*Hmmpf.* True enough." Irv glanced at the clock on the wall. "And I'll have Mari in the aftrernoons."

I listened to them talk about how he'd be babysitting his granddaughter in this kitchen while her mom was working. Her mom was Bess Mellits, the rec center's new director. Deanna's childcare room only took kids under age four, and Mari was six.

In a flash, the most brilliant out-of-the-box idea came to me. Hallie would be proud. Mr. Thompson, too.

I took a deep breath, trying to be bold like Hallie. "Excuse me, um, if you're not using the kitchen in the afternoon, would it be okay if I used it sometimes?"

I told Irv about needing a place to make two hundred bags of chips. I promised we wouldn't make any mess. I explained that Nai Nai dragged me here anyway. And I said Mari could help, if she wanted—

"Absolutely not. Out of the question!" Irv exploded before I'd finished.

I bit my lip, stung by his outburst. Hanging my head, I turned to go.

"Irv, really now!" Deanna scolded. "Don't run off, Jaye. What if both of you made a deal?"

"What kind of deal?" Irv glowered at her.

Deanna proposed that in exchange for Irv letting me and Hallie use the kitchen, I had to type his recipes for the cookbook. I nodded eagerly.

Irv stared at his laptop, then up at the ceiling for the longest time.

"Come on, Irv," Deanna pleaded for me.

He finally sighed. "Fine, but I have a lot of rules," he warned.

"I'm great at following rules," I promised.

I thanked him and raced back to Nai Nai. I pulled my phone from my hoodie pocket.

BIG surprise 4 u!

I texted Hallie.

got one 4 u 2!

She texted back.

mine's better

not even a little

what's yours?

come over now!!!!

u NEED 2 see it 2 believe it

CHAPTER 4
HALLIE

What I Had to Give Henry for His Help

– my tiny cube of shiny pyrite (I used my money to buy it at the museum gift shop)

– my gift card for a sundae at Scoops (I would've chosen mint chip ice cream with marshmallow sauce)

– my teal scooter (the wheels are going on another robot he's building)

"Let's get farming!" I bounced into Henry's doorway after school on Tuesday.

"One sec." My fifteen-year-old brother didn't look up. He was busy twisting a wire with a pair of pliers. Pushing aside a tangle of springs on his desk, he reached for a half-eaten cheese sandwich. He took a bite, chewing extra slowly.

"Henry! Mom's coming back in two hours. We need to do this *now*. You promised."

I'd traded all of those things in my list for Henry's help. But I knew it would be worth it. My idea was stupendous.

Henry finally stood. "Nice outfit."

"Why, thank you." After school, I'd changed into faded denim overalls, a bright green shirt, and my dad's floppy canvas fishing hat. I have a trunk plastered with travel stickers at the foot of my bed, and it's packed with assorted clothes and accessories. I wholeheartedly believe in dressing for the occasion.

Today I needed to look like a farmer.

Because Henry and I were making a mini cricket farm.

In our attic.

You see, Jaye and I need crickets to make our chips. We already learned that you can't just scoop up crickets from the yard to cook with, because there might be pesticides or other harmful stuff on them. And buying crickets from a pet store or through the mail gets expensive, especially since we needed a lot. (One thousand crickets cost like sixty dollars!) So, since I'm all about DIY, I figured I'd raise them myself.

Stupendous, right?

If I start with a handful of crickets and they mate and have babies and then those babies grow up and mate and have babies and so on, soon Jaye and I will have thousands of crickets. And they'd be totally organic 'cause I'm going to feed them only good stuff.

Which is another great selling point for our pitch.

I've been reading all about cricket farms on the internet. Usually the bugs are raised in big tubs in warehouses.

Except I'm doing it in our attic, because:

1. I don't have a warehouse.

2. Crickets like somewhere dark and warm.

3. Mom won't see it there.

Personally, I thought Mom would be cool with raising crickets, because she's always saying "roll up your sleeves and get your hands dirty," which means do stuff and don't just read about it. This summer she let me mash grapes with my bare feet to make grape juice! But Henry said breeding five hundred crickets—that's how many we bought to start— inside our house wouldn't fly with her. (Oh, that's punny! Get it? Crickets fly!) So I promised him I'd keep it a secret.

Henry grabbed an extra heat lamp from Randall's terrarium. "Okay, let's do this."

"You're going to be one happy lizard soon," I told Randall. I'd be supplying crickets for his dinner. That was another part of my deal with Henry. He wouldn't have to buy crickets any more to feed his pet lizard.

I'm a farmer for all creatures, big and small.

In the hall, Henry yanked the cord to open the ceiling hatch. He pulled the wobbly staircase down, and I climbed after him into the attic. Swirls of dust kicked up, tickling my nose.

The last rays of late afternoon sun filtered through a window at the far end of the attic. Our suitcases were piled near the stairs. Dad had taken the big blue one to a photography conference in Chicago yesterday. He'd be gone the whole week. He teaches nature photography at the local college, and he's writing a book on female photographers in the arctic. We've got a lot of snowy photos lying around our house.

Henry and I had already made a plan for when Dad got back. We'd act all helpful and return his suitcase up here for him. This way he wouldn't see what we were up to. Wouldn't see the crickets.

Henry walked to the middle of the attic and placed the

heat lamp beside a large, empty plastic storage tub. Our holiday ornaments had been dumped in a corner. Since his high school bus got home earlier than my bus, he'd already brought up everything we needed.

I opened my Listbook to double-check.

☑ 1 big storage bin with lid

☑ 1 heat lamp

☑ 2 plastic deli food containers with lids (hello, kitchen!)

☑ clean sponge (from the kitchen again)

☑ spritzer bottle of water (the mister mom uses for her plants)

☑ sawdust (Henry made some from wood)

☑ peat moss (from Dad's gardening stuff)

☑ empty egg cartons (got 2, ask Mom to make breakfast-for-dinner a lot more so we can get others)

☑ aluminum window screening ("borrowed" the spare screen that's been sitting in our garage forever)

☑ duct tape (from garage tool bench)

I eyed the bin. "It looks way too large."

"It's perfect, because it has high, smooth sides," Henry explained. "Crickets would use any grooves like ladders and scale the walls to escape."

I chuckled. "Can you imagine if they got loose?"

"Don't laugh. If our house gets infested with hundreds of jumping crickets, it's all over for you." He sliced his finger dramatically across his throat.

"You, too," I reminded him.

"Where's your little partner? Shouldn't she be here?"

"It's not Jaye's kind of project." On our class field trip, I'd been the only one brave enough to try a roasted cricket. People all over the world eat them, but Jaye had been freaked out. Now she's comfortable with cricket powder, but the handling-bugs part of our chips still gives her the creeps.

In BEE (that's what we all call Business Education and Entrepreneurship class), Mr. T taught us about division of labor. That means different people do different jobs.

I'd be our cricket farmer.

I showed Henry the instructions I'd printed. Then I scrubbed the bin while Henry cut small holes in the lid. He wore gloves and used special wire cutters to cut the window screen. Then he taped pieces of the screens over the holes. This allowed the crickets to breathe but kept them from escaping.

"What's that for?" I pointed to the sawdust he'd sprinkled on the bottom of the bin.

"Sawdust dries out poop." Henry grinned. "Even crickets poop."

I wrinkled my nose. "If you say so."

I placed the larger plastic deli container lined with peat moss into the bin. "This is the nursery where the crickets can lay their eggs."

I added a small container with a piece of wet sponge. Crickets need fresh water to survive. Outside, they drink from dew drops and raindrops. Here, they'd sip from the sponge. They could drown if I left out a bowl of water.

I slid in another small container for their food.

"I need to plan a super-fabulous menu." I explained to Henry that what crickets ate changed how they tasted. So if we fed them mint leaves, our cricket powder would have a minty flavor. If we fed them onions, it would taste onion-y.

"Let's give them fried chicken," he said.

"Crickets eat only plants, veggies, and fruits. Kind of like me." I've been a vegetarian for a year. Actually, now I'm an entotarian, because I eat bugs too.

"That's why you're always *bugging* me!" Henry cracked

himself up. His rumbling laugh echoed in the attic.

"These act like itty-bitty hotel rooms." I ignored his joke and placed the egg cartons inside the bin. The crickets would climb, hide, and live in them. "I want my guests to be nice and snug."

"I thought you were a farmer, not a hotel director."

"I'm both." Maybe I'd add a plastic name tag to my outfit, like they wore at hotel front desks. "I'm going to the kitchen. You get the crickets. Meet back here in five."

Henry gave a mock salute. It was fun being the boss of him.

I returned with apple slices sprinkled with cinnamon. It's my favorite snack. I placed them into the container.

Henry held the box of five hundred crickets we'd had shipped to us. I'd told Jaye I was using the money we'd saved to buy crickets. I didn't mention any of this.

"Are the guests ready to check in?" I asked. "My hotel is officially open."

Henry dumped half of the squirming brown crickets into the bin. The other half I'd freeze so we could make chips. We sealed the lid tight and turned on the heat lamp.

My phone pinged with a text from Jaye, and I told her to hurry over.

Henry returned to his room to do his homework. We agreed to check on our guests after dinner. It wasn't going to be easy sneaking up to the attic. Luckily, Dad wasn't around, so that only left Mom. One of us would have to distract her while the other cared for our critters.

While I waited for Jaye, I sat cross-legged by the bin and played music for the crickets from my phone. Did you know a cricket's ears are on its knees?

I'm filled with bug facts.

Jaye showed up, and I led her upstairs to show her my surprise. I pointed to the bin. "Ta-da!"

She looked confused.

She lifted a corner of the lid, peeked inside . . . and let

out a blood-curdling scream!

"*Shh!* You're scaring the guests." I pushed the lid closed.

"The *guests*? Hallie! They're crickets! Tons of crickets!"

I explained my plan. "I know I said think outside the box, but this is my think inside-the-bin stupendous solution to our supply problem."

Jaye hesitantly agreed it was pretty genius. "As long as the crickets stay in *your* house and not mine. I'm not touching them while they're alive."

Then she told me she'd gotten us a professional kitchen.

"But it comes with a grumpy old man?" I wasn't so sure about this.

"I'll deal with him. You deal with the crickets."

"You and me." I wiggled my fingers like antennae.

"We're slaying this. The Super Slayers!"

Jaye peeked out the window. "Uh-oh! Your mom's car is coming up the driveway."

"Go, go, go!" We raced out of the attic. I folded the stairs and closed the hatch, just as the front door opened.

"Hi, uh . . . Marika," Jaye said as we jogged downstairs. Jaye was still awkward about using my mom's first name like she'd asked her to.

"Hi, Jaye. I didn't know you were here. Hallie, what've you been up to?" She raised her eyebrows at my costume. "And why are you so . . . dusty?"

"Just trying out some clothes for the pitch competition—"

"Is that for your art?" Jaye pointed to the folded fabric my mom held. "Can I see?"

And just like that, Jaye got my mom talking art, which is her favorite thing in the whole world.

I flashed my partner a grateful smile.

CHAPTER 5
JAYE

"Let's start, folks," Mr. Thompson called from the back of his classroom on Wednesday afternoon. "We got a full house today."

I gazed about in wonder. Almost every seat was taken. When Hallie and I came up with the idea for the Pitch Club, I never thought so many other kids would join. But here they were, eager to build their businesses, even if they weren't moving ahead in the pitch competition like we were.

I watched Erica and Samara Matthews whisper and

giggle about Hallie's outfit. Today, Hallie had paired a yellow-and-white polka-dot shirt with a pink-and-red striped skirt. She was all about mixing patterns. I used to think her clothes were weird, too. Now that I know her, I realize they're just very Hallie.

Samara gave a little wave. I waved back, then pushed my hand into the pocket of my gray hoodie, hoping Hallie hadn't seen. It was hard figuring out where I fit in. I definitely wasn't friends with Erica and Samara the way I used to be, but I wasn't *not* friends with them, either.

"Jaye, ready?" Mr. Thompson ran his hand across his chin stubble.

I stood and tucked my hair behind my ears. My stomach twisted every time I ran the meetings. I still wasn't sure why Hallie decided I should be club president. I was more the club secretary type.

"Can we be in the hot seats today?" Owen Locke called out. He was creating an online video homework service.

Our meetings always began with a startup team sharing what they were doing. They sat in the hot seats, which were really two chairs dragged to the front, and we'd all give suggestions.

"It's . . ." I hesitated.

200 bags. 200 bags. 200 bags.

The words had been running in a loop in my brain all day. Even though Hallie wasn't worried, I was. I made a snap decision. We needed help before I could concentrate on anything else.

"Um, so today we're going to flip things. We'll do 'Mr. T. Talks,' and then we'll end the meeting with Owen and Vivi in the hot seats." I looked to Mr. Thompson. "Is that okay?"

"You're in charge." He grinned. "I assume you want to be first."

I nodded. There had to be some perks to being president, right?

For "Mr. T Talks," Mr. Thompson used his big chair as

a scooter, wheeling between startups to check in and solve problems. Each team went to a different part of the room to work until it was their turn with Mr. Thompson.

He rolled over to our desks first. I told him about the challenge and showed him the chart I'd made. I hated that it was still blank. (It turned out the five bags we'd sold before didn't count. We had to start fresh.)

# bags sold	to who	where

"We need a website to sell a lot of chips," I declared. "A fancy one."

"Websites are good," Mr. Thompson agreed, "but if you sell your chips that way, you have to pay to box and ship them. If it were me, I'd begin by selling locally. Here at school. Or around town."

Before becoming a teacher, Mr. Thompson owned his own advertising company. My dad says the best way to learn something is by having an expert show you.

"What about the park?" I suggested. "Sometimes the ice-cream truck comes by after soccer practice on Saturdays."

"That's good." Hallie's green eyes lit up. "We have

twenty bags of chips left from the last batch we made. We'll sell those and then make more."

Mr. Thompson wheeled away to help Erica and Lily Sullivan-Miller. They were deciding whether to include puffy stickers in their binder-decorating kits.

"How are the hotel guests doing?" I asked Hallie.

"Great!" Hallie beamed. "Chillin' and eating and crawling—"

"Yeah, yeah." I cringed. I couldn't bear to think about all that crawling. "When are the baby crickets coming?"

"It's too soon for that. They just checked in." Hallie tipped her head. "It's actually really tricky to go see them. I've got to wait till my mom clears out—"

"Hey, Jaye. What do you think of this?" Ava Baltimore thrust a sketch for a bike helmet in front of me. It had one peacock feather sprouting from the top.

I studied it. Ava and her partner, Luke Grasing, were making personalized bike helmets. "What if you used a whole bunch of feathers instead? They'd go all flowy when you ride."

Ava loved my idea. We talked about the number of feathers to use, until Hallie cleared her throat loudly. Then she cleared it again. She wasn't even trying to hide that she wanted Ava gone.

"That was rude," I said, once Ava took the hint.

"What? My throat was dry."

Then Jazmina and Samara came by to see if the logo they drew was good. (Yes!) Dion and Sophia had me choose the color of their labels. (The white with the royal blue border.) Maddie and Noah asked if I liked the name of their company. (Not so much.)

Each time Hallie shooed them away. "Us first," she finally told me. "We need to make a plan for selling our chips at the park."

"Okay," I agreed. But before the meeting had finished, two more teams wanted my opinion. Somehow they all thought because I was club president, I knew what I was doing.

I didn't. But I still liked helping.

Hallie frowned at me, which was weird because she's always smiling.

"What's wrong?" I asked.

"Nothing. I just want you to pay attention to *our* business. You and me."

I blinked several times, confused. What was she talking about? I was paying attention to Chirps.

I was about to get angry, but then I wondered: Instead of our *business*, did she really mean *her*? Had I been ignoring Hallie? I didn't think so.

"I am," I assured her. I made my eyes go wide and gave her an exaggerated stare. "Total attention."

She smiled big.

CHAPTER 6
HALLIE

Businesses Built by Best Friends

- Ben & Jerry's Ice Cream
- Microsoft
- Apple
- Airbnb
- Rent the Runway

I scooted in beside Jaye the next day at lunch.

"Hey." She smiled then turned to Ava and Sophia DuPre to finish the story she was telling. It had something to do with their Language Arts class.

Jaye and I only had BEE together. I wished we shared other classes.

They all laughed, and I smiled, too. I used to sit at a random table in the lunchroom and read my book. I was fine with that. I'm okay being on my own. But I liked sitting with Jaye better.

Jaye used to sit at the popular kids table until she'd had the blow up with Spencer. She made a big point of moving to a different table, which I think was super brave. She could've probably stayed.

But she wanted to be with me.

Or she felt bad that her pitch partner sat alone.

I wasn't quite sure which it was.

After Jaye moved tables, Sophia, Ava, and Jazmina Perez

did, too. So now it was the five of us. Ava was the chattiest of the group. I really liked how she sprinkled gold glitter on the dozens of long box braids that covered her head. Sophia was the quietest. She played violin in the school orchestra with Jaye and knew all these cool facts about what to do if you're trapped in an avalanche or in a sinking car in a lake. Jazmina was the tallest kid in our grade and really athletic, which I'm so not. She played soccer with Jaye, but she also played basketball and lacrosse.

But they sat here for Jaye, not me. I knew that.

I didn't always sit alone. At least not in elementary school. Back then, I had a best friend. Zara and I met in a toddler playgroup, and it'd been the two of us together every day since. We went on treasure hunts in our yards, molded papier-mâché masks of our faces, and stirred up magical no-bake candy.

But Zara's family moved to Canada this summer. Leaving me alone, until Jaye and I started working together.

But now I wasn't sure what the rules to making a new best friend were.

"Erica and Spencer are for sure breaking up," Ava announced. She always knew all the gossip. "I heard they had a fight."

"About what?" Jaye asked.

"He keeps answering her texts with one word. Cool . . . yeah . . . haha," Jazmina reported.

Ava rolled her eyes. "It's like he doesn't care about her."

"How rude," Sophia agreed.

"Nah, Spencer's just awkward about stuff like that," Jaye said, defending him. She was always doing that.

"Lily invited both of them to her party," Ava pointed out. "*That's* awkward."

"Wait, Lily is having a boy/girl party?" Jazmina's brown eyes went wide.

"Yeah," Ava said. "But only girls are staying for the sleepover part."

They started talking about what to wear. I ate my almond-butter-and-banana sandwich silently. Lily hadn't invited me. No surprise there.

Then I noticed Jaye wasn't saying anything. Was she not invited, either? Was that even possible?

The almond butter caught in my throat. If Jaye hadn't started hanging out with me, she'd definitely be going to that party. This was my fault.

She'd chosen me, and now they were leaving her out.

I tried to read her face. Zara and I had this best friend thing. When we were eight, we named it The Connection. It's when you're so in tune with each other you don't have to speak because with one glance you know each other's thoughts.

I had no idea what Jaye was thinking.

"Hey, guess what?" I told her about Henry's newest robot. He was programming its long arm to pick up a dirty sock from his floor and drop it into his hamper. "What if he could program it to put food into the crickets' bin? Wouldn't that be cool?"

I babbled on to block out the other girls. I didn't want Jaye to have to hear them talk about Lily's party.

Jaye nodded at me. But she was still listening to Jazmina and Sophia *and* stealing glances over at Spencer and Erica's table.

She couldn't help herself. Jaye still believed she was like Erica and Lily and all those other "color-inside-the-lines" girls. That's what my mom used to call them. She says that kids like me who aren't afraid to splatter paint and toss glitter; who are different and creative; are the ones who change the world. We're the ones with "spark."

Jaye has spark, too.

I knew it the same way a butterfly recognizes another butterfly in a swarm of moths.

I sighed. I liked it better when it was just the two of us.

CHAPTER 7
JAYE

"Go, Bryar!" I sprinted up the right side of the field on Saturday afternoon. Bryar dribbled the ball up the left side. The score was tied 3–3 in the final minutes of the game. Bryar was the fastest on the Comets, and I pushed myself to keep pace.

Bryar dodged the Falcons' defender, searching for an open pass opportunity. I crossed, but Jazmina, our center midfielder, found a pocket first. Bryar rocketed the ball. Jazmina settled it, skirting a Falcon defender. A second

Falcon defender raced toward her, but I blocked her path. In that instant, Jazmina kicked and GOAL!!!

We'd won!

The whole team circled Jazmina. Parents cheered from the sidelines, and Jazmina's dad chanted her name. Others whooped for Bryar's assist.

I didn't look over. Mama and Baba work on Saturdays. And today, Nai Nai had dropped me off then drove Eddie to a pre-tournament match somewhere. I mopped my sweaty face with the bottom of my light-blue jersey. I wondered if he'd bring home another trophy—we had two shelves in the family room filled with tiny shiny guys on pedestals holding racquets.

"Woo-hoo! Jaye! Yay, Jaye! You blocking machine!!"

I whirled around. Who was cheering for me?

Hallie! I jogged over.

She gave me a wide grin and a hug. "You're really good."

"No, I'm not. I mean, I'm fine but—"

"You looked amazing to me. Own it." Hallie gazed around at the three soccer fields, the baseball diamond, the packed walking trails, and the playground. "I can't believe how many people are here. Brookdale Park's the perfect place to sell our chips."

I grabbed my sweats from the side and followed her to a stretch of grass by the parking lot. Her mom had already set up a little folding table and was attaching the sign we'd drawn at Pitch Club.

EAT WHAT BUGS YOU!
CHIRPS
CHIPS
GOOD FOR YOUR YUMMY, TOO!
1 BAG = $4.00

"Hey there, Jaye." A yawn escaped as Hallie's mom gave me a hug. They were a very huggy family.

"I love your skirt." It looked like it was made from twenty men's neckties all sewn together. She'd paired it with a fraying ivory fisherman's sweater, white sneakers, and beaded earrings that poked out from her long honey-brown hair. I suddenly wished I knew how to sew. And bead cool earrings.

"Oh, this thing? I made it years ago. My found-materials clothing phase." She yawned again. "Excuse me. Bad night. Our old house has been making the weirdest noises."

"What kind of noises?"

"Jaye—" Hallie grabbed my elbow and jerked me to the other side of the table. "Stand over here and wave down customers."

I twisted back to keep talking to her mom. Marika sells

paintings and sculptures in small galleries throughout the state. She's the first real artist I've met. My parents both work in a biochemistry lab. Their work is very precise. Very serious. Just like them.

"The noises?" Marika tilted her head, pondering my question. "They're high-pitched. A chittering—is that a word? Otherworldly. My friend Francie suspects a spirit is passing through, but that's Francie for you. But I *am* working on this collage of dead people, so maybe—"

"A spirit? Like a ghost?"

"Jaye!" Hallie's voice grew more insistent. "We're missing out on customers. Hey, want some chips?" She called after a family walking a golden retriever.

"Can you believe we get haunted by a ghost just when Stan's away?" Marika sighed. "I left my coffee in the car. I'll let you girls do your thing."

As soon as her mom was out of earshot, Hallie exclaimed. "Don't let her talk about *that!*"

"About the poltergeist in your house?"

"Hello? We don't have a ghost. We've got crickets. Really loud chirping crickets."

"Oh." Now I understood. "That's bad."

"You have no idea. You know what two or three crickets sound like in your backyard on a summer's night? Now multiply that by two hundred and then shove 'em all together in an attic. They really get singing. Turns out they're nocturnal." Now Hallie yawned. "But I'm not."

"Isn't it only the males that rub their front wings together to sing? So it should only be about half of them making noise. I mean, you did get half and half, right?"

"I don't know. It sure doesn't sound like half." Hallie wore a panicked look. "Henry and I have been putting on fans and playing music to muffle the noise. I'm not sure how long Francie's ghost theory will hold up."

"What are these?" A dad in an orange knit cap called out. He picked up one of the bags we'd lined up on the table.

Hallie did an amazing job telling him about our chips. He bought two bags.

I pulled out my chart and recorded the sale. We were on the chart! A few more parents stopped by, and we sold six more bags.

Across the parking lot, Erica's unmistakable laugh made me look up. She, Samara, and Lily climbed out of her mom's car. They all wore cute sweaters and sporty leggings. I pulled my sweaty hair free from my hair band and tried to fluff it, but it didn't matter—they didn't notice us. They were headed toward one of the upper fields.

Hailey saw me watching them. "I'm glad you're not going to Lily's party. We can do something fun together. What about tie-dye?"

Before I had a chance to say anything, a group of loud ten-year-old boys in black-and-yellow soccer jerseys surrounded our table.

"Four dollars?" The tallest boy's cheeks were still red

from his game. "The ice cream guy only charges two dollars for a cone."

"Yeah, your chips cost too much," one of his teammates agreed.

"Let's get ice cream." The first boy started to lead them away.

"Hold up! Just for you, each bag is two dollars," Hallie called. "And, trust me, you'll be able to share way cooler photos eating *cricket* chips than a boring ice-cream cone."

Score! The boys bought eight bags.

"Only two dollars?" Bryar Benson's mom asked, stepping up with Bryar. "We'll take a bag."

I started to say it'd only been a special price for the boys, but Hallie had already snatched her money. Then she grabbed a marker and changed the price on our sign.

Bryar arched one eyebrow. "I charge *six dollars* for my muffins, because they're gourmet and all natural and organic."

"Our chips are all-natural and organic, too," Hallie retorted.

"Yeah, but I'll be making a whole lot more money than you will," she bragged.

My brain started spinning. Had we just made a big mistake? No, the challenge was the amount we sold, not the money we made. Unless . . . I tried to do the math in my head. If we sold each bag for only two dollars, would we make enough money to cover what the ingredients and the packaging cost us—even with Hallie's cricket hotel? I didn't think so.

When Bryar left, Hallie and I discussed changing the price. We settled on three dollars.

We planned to set up a bigger table in the park next Saturday. We'd tie on a bunch of balloons and play peppy tunes. We had enough frozen crickets to bake sixty bags of chips this week. We'd sold seventeen bags in twenty minutes today. Next weekend we'd blow through sixty bags, no problem.

# bags sold	to who	where
17	families and soccer players	Brookdale Park

"What're you selling here?"

A barrel-chested police officer in a dark-blue uniform examined our chips with interest. His nametag read: M. COSTAS.

"Chips we made with cricket powder." Hallie launched into her dynamo sales speech. "We're about to raise the price again, but since you're a first responder, you can buy them for two dollars—"

Officer Costas didn't let her finish. He pointed at Hallie, then at me. "You need to pack up and leave the park now. I'm officially shutting you down."

CHAPTER 8
HALLIE

"Wait, what? You can't shut us down. This is for a school project!" I cried.

"Doesn't matter." Officer Costas ran his hand along his buzzed black hair. "It's against the law to sell food in the park."

"Says who? The ice-cream guy sells food." I planted my hands on my hips. "Besides, it's a free country."

I looked to Jaye to back me up, but she'd gone pale and shaky.

"The ice-cream truck vendor was required to get a permit from the town and a food-selling license from the health department," said Officer Costas. "If you don't have a permit, you have to leave."

"What's happening?" My mom hurried over as a crowd started to form. I groaned. Finally, we had a crowd, and now we couldn't sell any chips.

Officer Costas explained the town's rules. And, boy, there were lots of them! First off, we needed to pay money for this permit thing. And even if we could afford and were granted the permit, all our food had to be labeled "made in a home kitchen," and we had to have all the ingredients listed for people to see. And we'd even have to get our kitchen inspected.

"B-b-but we're just kids!" I sputtered.

It turns out our age didn't matter. Officer Costas said the town was protecting its citizens. They couldn't just let anyone sell food made at home without being sure it was cooked in a clean place, handled properly, and the ingredients were safe to eat. I explained that Jaye and I were super clean. I'm *always* washing my hands. I wanted to tell him how I've been giving the crickets in the attic clean filtered water every day and fresh cinnamon apples, but Mom was standing right there so I left that part out.

I kept trying to argue. Then Mom rested her hand on my arm. "It's time to go."

Mom marches in every climate change, racial equality, and women's rights protest—she even took a bus to

Washington, DC, once. If she wasn't fighting back, it meant she agreed with Officer Costas. My shoulders slumped.

Selling in the park had been the perfect plan.

What would we do now?

My phone buzzed Monday morning and, for a moment, I wasn't sure where I was. Rubbing the sleep from my eyes, I tried to bring everything into focus. Goldfish swimming lazily in a glass bowl. Crumpled Halloween candy wrappers. Gauzy white curtain. The little green origami crickets Jaye had made lined up on the windowsill.

I was in my room. I remembered crawling back into bed around 3:00 a.m. It was now 6:20 a.m.

And my dad was calling. I answered groggily.

"Hi, monkey. I miss you." Dad sounded bright and energetic—the opposite of how I felt. For the last two nights, after Mom had gone to bed, I'd sneaked up into the attic. The crickets were at it full force, chirping loudly and skittering inside the bin. I kept the lid closed—it was tricky to open it without Henry there, because they liked to jump out. Instead, I made a nest of blankets and curled up beside the bin.

My plan was to calm them down. And shut them up.

I tried whispering fairy tales.

Didn't work.

I recited multiplication tables. Then state capitals.

Still didn't work.

Then I played Bob Marley's "One Love" and they went quiet. Who knew? So I spent the night spinning the song on repeat for my hotel of crickets.

Now I drifted off as Dad told me about his conference.

"Your mom called in the middle of the night. She thinks the house is haunted." Dad continued, "At one point, she even thought she heard music. But then—"

"That was me. I couldn't sleep." Technically, this was true.

"Okay, that explains something. Did you hear the noises, too?"

"When I sleep, I don't hear anything." Also true.

"Listen, do me a favor. Let your mom sleep in, okay? Can you and your brother make breakfast quietly and get yourselves on the bus?"

"Of course."

I planned to be long gone before Mom woke up.

 Songs Crickets Sing

 1. Love Song (Cricket trying to get another cricket's attention.)

2. Fight Song (Cricket getting pumped up to brawl.)

 3. Warning Song (Antennae up! Danger's near!)

At the end of fourth period, I waited at the desk of Mrs. Stein, my science teacher, while everyone else raced into the crowded hall.

"I have questions," I announced.

"You always have questions, Hallie." She glanced at me over the rims of her cat's-eye glasses. "About the homework?"

"About how to quiet crickets at night." I was exhausted. Midnight DJ sessions needed to end.

"November's late for crickets," she remarked.

"Outside, sure. But I have a farm. Well, a hotel. Or maybe now it's a dance party. In my attic."

"Oh, Hallie." She sucked her teeth. "What are you up to?"

So I told her.

She didn't have any books about crickets, but she found a good website. It turns out the best way to silence crickets is to blast them with cold air, because crickets stop chirping around seventy degrees Fahrenheit. But—and here was the problem—they needed it to be warm to mate and have babies.

Should I chill them out so Mom wouldn't freak out?

Or heat them up so we'd get the crickets we needed?

"All the chirping may be because they're getting ready to lay eggs in a week," Mrs. Stein said. Her fifth period class had started to file in.

"That's it! The cricket's love song!" I exclaimed, remembering my list. I could keep them quiet for one more week.

"Then it takes another eight days for the eggs to hatch." Mrs. Stein clicked off the screen and stood.

Two more weeks! My stomach dropped. That was too long.

I needed to talk to Henry. It was time to fess up to Mom.

CHAPTER 9
JAYE

I kept telling Nai Nai it was safe to leave us at the rec center's kitchen. Even Hallie, who didn't understand my grandma's Mandarin, tried to convince her. But Nai Nai always thinks something bad will happen.

Finally, Irv shuffled in, holding the hand of a small girl with blond chin-length hair and big gray eyes. I figured she was Mari, his granddaughter.

"I won't let them burn the place down," was all he grumbled when I introduced Nai Nai.

Not exactly words of comfort.

Then Irv bent and tenderly cleaned Mari's hands with a wipe and tied her shoe. And Nai Nai agreed we could stay.

"Let's cook!" Hallie quickly told him how we now baked our chips instead of frying them, but Irv cut her off mid-story.

"First rule: silence." He frowned. "This is how it's going to work. You prepare your batter or dough or bugs or whatever you do. I handle the oven. Rule two: I don't help in any other way. Then you type my recipes. You clean up. And I mean *scrub*. And you leave. Two hours exactly and then out."

I nodded eagerly. Using this kitchen—and his bowls and baking sheets and cabinet of spices—was huge for us.

"I get to cook, too." Mari tugged the hem of her grandfather's plaid shirt.

"That's fine. We got her," I assured him. I really wanted Irv to like us.

Irv made us wash our hands and tie on stiff white aprons. After preheating the oven, he sat on a stool to write a grocery list for his cooking classes.

Hallie pulled the Ziploc bag of frozen crickets from her backpack. Mr. Thompson had let us store them for the day in the teachers' room freezer. We'd put on a sticky note that said: **DO NOT EAT!** because you never know when a teacher's going to get hungry.

"Want to see?" Hallie asked Irv.

Irv didn't lift his head. "No. Rule three: You do your thing. I'll do mine."

"Can I play music?" Hallie liked to cook with tunes blasting.

"No," he repeated. "Rule one: Don't make noise."

"What if music's my thing?" she whispered to me.

"*Shhh.*" I placed the corn masa and vegetable oil on the counter. Then I lined up the spices we'd need: black pepper, salt, paprika, garlic powder, cumin, chili powder.

"Ohhh!" Mari gasped when Hallie dumped the frozen crickets onto a baking pan. "Are they dead?"

"Yep. Frigid cold kills them," Hallie explained. "That's why we froze 'em."

"*Hmpf,* ridiculous." Irv muttered a few times. We pretended not to hear.

Hallie made up a song about crickets in her attic, and Mari sang along. Irv stole curious glances.

"No one's eating these," he declared, when he slid the pan into the oven for us.

"You're wrong. Go to Mexico or Thailand, and you'll find everyone eating them. They've been doing it for thousands of years. And now crickets are the future of food." Hallie turned to me. "Hey, that's a good line for the pitch."

"Well, I don't live in—" Irv started.

"Why don't I type up some recipes?" I wanted to stop Irv and Hallie from arguing. "And Mari can help color a new poster."

"Poster for where?" Hallie turned to Irv. "Did you know I wrote the mayor a letter?" She told him about the town's rules and what had happened at the park. But he wasn't listening. He stacked a pile of handwritten recipe cards next to the laptop.

I picked up the top one. Tilting my head at his slanted writing, I typed a recipe for *Spicy Mac-n-Cheese.* It sounded pretty good.

"We'll find a new spot." I told Hallie.

Hallie continued to talk—about the cricket farm, slogans for our chips, the book she had to read for Language Arts. She was clearly breaking Irv's number one rule, but he didn't stop her. I think because Mari happily chattered back.

I typed six more recipes.

After an hour went by, the roasted crickets were ready to come out of the oven. They looked like shriveled up raisins. Once they cooled, we poured them into a bag and gave them the "shake and bake." Shaking makes the wings and antennae fall off. Trust me, no one wants a wing caught between their teeth! It was easy to separate them out, because they fell to the bottom of the bag—the same way the little seeds and bits in trail mix collect at the bottom.

Then Hallie used the rolling pin to crush the roasted crickets.

"*Yeesh!* You'll be here all day if you do it that way." Irv pulled out a food processor. "Grind them with this."

Hallie raised an eyebrow. "I thought you didn't want to help us."

"I don't. I want my kitchen back."

We quickly pulverized the crickets into a fine powder. Then we combined the powder with corn masa and hot water.

"It's like Play-Doh." Mari giggled as she helped us form the dough into balls.

We flattened the dough balls with the rolling pin and brushed them with oil. Then Hallie and I huddled around the spices.

"What're you doing?" Mari tugged at my sweatshirt. "Let me see!"

"No looking. We're blending our top secret seasoning mix." When we'd first created the recipe, it took a super long time to get the spices right.

"We're just like KFC," Hallie said. "Except no chicken."

"What are you talking about?" Irv demanded.

Hallie explained. "KFC's eleven herbs and spices recipe is top secret, too. It's written on a piece of paper and locked in a bank vault. The vault's surrounded by security cameras and motion detectors. They have one company blend one part of the mixture and a different company blend the other half. This way no one can steal the secret recipe."

"You think I'm going to steal your recipe?" Irv snorted.

"Jaye's making a cookbook for you, isn't she? Seems to me it'd be good to include a healthy Earth-friendly snack like ours." Hallie shrugged. "Just sayin'."

She did have a point. I'd just typed up *Extra-Cheesy Nacho Beef Skillet*. Nothing healthy about that.

"*Humpf*," Irv grunted.

After we sprinkled on the seasoning and cut the tortillas into triangles, he slid the trays in the oven to bake.

I went back to typing recipes.

Hallie played a clean-up game with Mari.

Irv sat on his stool, scowling.

"Hey, Nai Nai!" Hallie called, when my grandma came back with Eddie.

Nai Nai flashed her crooked smile. For all the years I'd been friends with Spencer, she'd never smiled like that at him. And Spencer had kept his distance from my grandma. I think he was scared of her. She can be a bit intense. But when Hallie showed up at my house after we were made pitch partners, she somehow knew that Nai Nai—with her wide wrinkled forehead, cap of silver hair, and serious stare—was way more cozy than she looked. And Nai Nai understood immediately that Hallie overflowed with sparkly change-the-world ideas.

"We must go," Nai Nai told us. Eddie was hungry, and she wanted to make dinner before my parents got home from work.

"Can't Eddie wait?" I asked. The chips had just come out of the oven. They needed to cool before we could divide them into bags.

"Listen to your grandmother. Your two hours are up," Irv said.

"But our chips—" Hallie started.

"Whoa, we have a problem." Irv was looking at his computer now. "You only typed nine recipes."

"I can finish them now." I glanced at Nai Nai. She shook her head at me. "Or I can—"

Irv didn't wait for me to finish. "Here's the plan. You both go home. I'll wait for your bug chips to cool, then put them in a container to stay fresh. You come back another day. You finish typing the cookbook like you promised, and then I'll give you your chips."

"What? You're holding onto our chips?" Hallie sounded as shocked as I felt.

"Yes. That way I know you'll come back." Irv folded his arms. "We made a deal, remember?"

"You won't eat them?" Hallie didn't trust him.

"Trust me. There's no way I'll eat your chips."

What could we do? A few minutes later, we climbed into Nai Nai's car empty-handed.

Hallie turned to me. "I can't believe we just left the only chips we have—made with the only crickets we had money to buy—with a grouchy guy who doesn't like us or our chips."

Would we ever see them again?

CHAPTER 10
HALLIE

"It'll be okay," Nai Nai told us as she drove. "That man, he has a knife mouth but a tofu heart."

"You're saying Irv's squishy on the inside?" Jaye asked.

"No way." I leaned forward. "That guy has a peach pit for a heart. Actually, I bet it's smaller. Like a popcorn kernel."

"It's a-*maize*-ing how *corny* that is." Jaye grinned.

"Ohhh, two-for-one pun!" She instantly got me into a better mood.

As Nai Nai steered through the center of town, I filled

Jaye in about what Mrs. Stein said about waiting two more weeks for baby crickets.

"That's assuming your mom lets you keep the hotel," Jaye pointed out. "And we'll have to cook the grown-up crickets sooner than that. The pitch competition is in two and a half weeks."

"We could buy more," I suggested.

"With what money?" Jaye asked.

"In Mr. T's class, we learned banks give loans to small businesses," I reminded her.

"To kids?" Jaye sounded doubtful.

"I can loan money like a bank," Nai Nai offered. "How much?"

"You're the best!" I would've hugged Nai Nai but she was hunched over the steering wheel, peering into the early evening darkness. She'd just turned down my long driveway. The headlights illuminated the outdoor sculptures my mom had made.

"One of the rules of Pitch is that we can't take money from our parents," Jaye explained.

Nai Nai answered in Mandarin.

"She said grandmas are different," Jaye translated. "But I'm telling her we don't want to get in trouble with the judges."

"Who's that?" Eddie pointed out the window.

A white van was parked in front of my house. Red letters on the van said PESTS-BEE-GONE.

Eddie read aloud the slogan on the van: "We wave goodbye to bugs."

"Is that . . . is that an exterminator?" Jaye whispered.

A rush of panic surged through my body. I swallowed hard. *Oh no! No, no, no.*

I opened the car door and sprinted across the gravel drive. I burst through the front door. "Hello? Mom?"

I heard muffled voices. Then footsteps above.

I raced upstairs.

The attic hatch hung open.

Thick-soled black boots were making their way down the wooden stairs.

I froze as a man in light-blue coveralls appeared. He held my large plastic bin.

"I sprayed them to stun them. I'll just take this out to the truck now," he called to someone behind him.

"What did you spray on them?" I cried. "Tell me!"

The exterminator gave me a hard, quizzical look.

"That's mine!" I lunged for the bin. But he held tight.

"Are you sure you got them all?" Mom appeared on the stairs.

"You can't take them! They're crickets. For our chips." I reached again for the bin, but he still held on.

"Hallie! Why were they in our attic—" Mom began.

"Please, Mom. I have it under control." My voice caught.

Her tone turned frosty. "I don't think you do. You know I haven't been sleeping. Today, I realized the noise was coming from above. I was too petrified to open the door myself, certain the attic was swarming with who knows what kind of creatures. I called the exterminator, and he discovers a bin of crickets. Crickets! It was *you* all along."

"We were breeding them," I said softly.

"This was your idea too, Jaye?"

I whirled around. Jaye had followed me into the house. She hovered at the top of the stairs and shot me a sympathetic look.

"Not Jaye. Henry," I told my mom.

I glanced toward Henry's bedroom. The door was open. That meant he was still at his tutoring job.

Mom rubbed her temples. "I can't believe this. What if they'd gotten out?"

"I'm sorry." The disappointment in her eyes made me want to curl up and cry.

"Should I still take it?" The exterminator lifted the bin.

"Definitely."

"No."

Mom and I spoke over each other.

I was about to plead for more time. But then I remembered what I'd heard the exterminator say. "What did you spray in the bin? A chemical?"

He nodded.

I locked eyes with Jaye. We couldn't use crickets that had been swimming in chemicals for our chips. My hotel was officially out of business.

Jaye and I sat together on the top stair. We watched the exterminator and Mom head out the front door with the crickets.

"Are you going to be in trouble?" Jaye asked.

"Probably." There'd be a lecture, for sure, when my dad came home tonight.

"You know, I don't think it would've worked out, anyway." Jaye bumped her shoulder up against mine. "It's like in *Charlotte's Web* when Fern doesn't want to kill Wilbur. You shouldn't cook with crickets you've been singing to and feeding home-cooked snacks."

"That's true." I had grown strangely fond of my little guests.

"Everything's such a mess." Jaye started to twirl her hair. "We've got no place to sell, no chips, and now no crickets."

"Don't think like that," I said. "Does the world need another blueberry muffin or hot sauce? I think not. But a way to feed lots of people that doesn't destroy our planet? We will figure out a way to make it happen!"

Jaye gave me a half smile. "So we just need to work out the bugs?"

"Exactly! And I like how you're still punny, even when you're worried."

I told Jaye that someday we'd be celebrated. We'd be on one of those Women Who Changed the World lists. I was sure of it.

 Fab Female-Founded Food Companies

Pepperidge Farms (pizza goldfish rule!)

Kikkoman (started in 1600s Japan by a soy sauce girl boss!)

Auntie Anne's (cinnamon sugar pretzel is my fave!)

Stacy's Pita Chips (Stacy sold her company for $250 MILLION!!!) **YUM!**

Chirps (Hallie & Jaye ignite a global food revolution!)

GIRL POWER!

CHAPTER 11
JAYE

Lining up the edges of the thin violet origami paper, my fingernail creased the center fold. I bent the corners back.

Fold, flip, fold, turn. I relaxed into the familiar rhythm.

I'd started doing origami this summer. I began with simple birds. Last week, I folded a super tricky giraffe. My plan is to make every animal on the planet. I already have a box stuffed with hundreds of swans, tigers, turtles, dolphins, and elephants in my closet. My own Noah's Ark. Except there's way more than two of each animal.

I slowed for two reverse folds. I didn't want this little paper rabbit to have lopsided ears.

The house was silent, except for the distant rumble of the washing machine. Nai Nai was down in our basement doing laundry. Eddie and I had had our cello lessons with Mrs. Chen right after school. Then Mama had picked up Eddie and driven him to the tennis courts.

She wouldn't let me come along. She said homework came first.

So Irv had to wait. Chirps had to wait.

But homework didn't come first for Eddie with the tournament coming up. It was so unfair. I was creating a business. Getting ready for a big pitch competition.

Mama said tennis could change Eddie's future. But Chirps could change mine, too.

I wished Hallie were here. Mama could use one of Hallie's *bee-lieve* talks. Then maybe she'd understand.

I put the little rabbit aside and started on my math

worksheet, angrily tapping my pencil on the kitchen table.

Then I spotted Spencer through the window, practicing layups in his driveway. He dribbled five times toward the hoop. He spun right, netting the ball. Then he sprinted back toward the line.

I smiled. We'd made up that drill together.

I hadn't hung out with Spencer since he'd stolen our idea and been so horrible to me and Hallie last month. I still hadn't forgiven him for that. But I was tired of being so angry.

Plus, I felt like shooting hoops.

I called out to Nai Nai that I needed to ask Spencer about the homework. Then I walked across the street. If

Spencer was surprised to see me, he didn't say anything. He passed me the ball.

I tried a free throw but missed. He caught the rebound. We fell into our usual rhythm. We'd lived across the street from each other since kindergarten. His house and driveway were as familiar as my own.

"How's Chirps?" he asked after a while.

"Fine," I said warily. I was surprised he hadn't made a snarky remark about Hallie. Or bugs.

"I told Uncle Gabe about it. He thinks it's cool. He says you guys are innovators."

So that was it. Spencer idolized his uncle. Uncle Gabe had designed a popular game app that he'd sold for a lot of money. If Uncle Gabe thought Chirps was cool, then Spencer thought so, too.

"He said you need to let people know about it." Spencer chased the ball down.

"We're trying." I told him about the email Hallie had

just gotten from Mayor Godfrey. The mayor had suggested that instead of a public place, we set up our stand in our front yard and sell there.

"Here?" Spencer laughed.

"I know, right?" No cars ever drove down our small dead-end street.

"Uncle Gabe lives in a super-tall building in New York City with a thousand apartments. If you lived there, you could set up in the lobby and get all those people to buy your chips," Spencer said.

"But I don't live there. I live here," I pointed out.

"Stinks for you." Spencer caught the rebound then netted his throw.

"Tell me about it." I dribbled the ball back.

"You going to Lily's party?"

"Yeah, I guess." I felt guilty that I was invited and Hallie wasn't. I'd thought about saying something to Lily, seeing if Hallie could come, but then decided it was awkward. They weren't friends. Besides, Hallie wouldn't want to go. She didn't like that group. "I heard you and Erica are going to the party together."

"Together how?"

"Like as a couple."

His face reddened. "I don't know. Maybe. I don't want to talk about that." He stole the ball from me and raced in for a layup.

"Jaye! Is that you?" Spencer's mom pushed open the back door. She tossed a bag of garbage in the bin then hurried over to hug me tight.

"Hi, Mrs. Montan." I inhaled her familiar warmth and the scent of sugar. "I smell your Oreo cheesecake cupcakes." They're my favorite. She always made them for special occasions and class parties.

"I've been baking up a storm for the PTA sale." She took my hand in both of hers and tugged me toward the door. "Have a taste."

"Seriously, Mom? We're shooting hoops here," Spencer said.

Mrs. Montan shared a knowing grin with me. "Here we go again, Jaye."

It had become a running joke. Ever since we were little, Mrs. Montan would occasionally swoop in and "borrow me" from Spencer. She had three sons, and she sometimes craved "girl time." It used to make Spencer really upset. He once locked me in his closet so his mom couldn't find me.

"Actually, I need to get back," I told her. "I have homework."

"You never come around anymore. We miss you." Mrs. Montan smoothed my staticky hair. "I'll grab you one for the road."

"Me, too!" Spencer called after her.

When she returned, Mrs. Montan said, "We're expecting a huge crowd at the bake sale before the school meeting. The superintendent is showcasing plans for the new addition."

"These will sell out fast." I cradled the cupcake in my hand.

"So would chips." Spencer spewed Oreo crumbs as he spoke.

"Chips?" His mom was confused.

"Cricket chips. The ones Jaye's making for Mr. Thompson's class," he said. "Can she sell them there?"

I was as confused as Mrs. Montan. "At the PTA bake sale?"

"Why not? The PTA sells cupcakes baked at home, so why not chips? And you don't need permission from the town. Just my mom." He crossed his arms, clearly pleased with himself. Mrs. Montan was PTA president, after all.

"The thing is, kids, our bake sale raises money to pay for school programs," she said. "All money earned must go back to the school. It can't land in Jaye's pocket."

"What if Jaye gives the money she makes to the PTA?" Spencer asked.

I considered this. We still needed to pay Henry back and now buy crickets. But, selling 183 bags of chips to complete the pitch challenge was way more important. And Mrs. Montan said there'd be a huge crowd. It was the perfect place!

"We can totally do that." I couldn't wait to tell Hallie.

Mrs. Montan gave me the green light. "Thank you so much!" I beamed at her.

"My boy gets the credit." She wrapped her arm around Spencer's shoulder, but he wiggled free.

I considered Spencer for a moment. "It's a great idea," I told him.

"Whatever." He swished the free throw.

I turned to go then stopped. "I forgot to ask. When's the bake sale?"

"Tomorrow night." Mrs. Montan smiled.

Oh no! I had to get our chips from Irv, and fast!

CHAPTER 12
HALLIE

"We're back!" I called out to Irv the next afternoon.

"Lucky me," he grumbled. He was trying to stuff large bags of shredded cheese and tubs of salsa inside the refrigerator.

Mari ran over to us, her little face crinkling with delight, and gave an excited hello.

"Sorry we couldn't come yester—" Jaye started.

"Where are our chips?" I demanded, getting right to it.

On the drive over, Jaye had asked me to please *bee* kind

to him. "Nai Nai always says 'You catch more flies with honey than vinegar.'"

"I don't want to catch flies," I'd told her. "I want our chips back."

The bake sale was in a few hours. Jaye told me the story about how she'd spotted Mrs. Montan in her driveway yesterday, and had gone over and talked her into it. Brilliant!

But we still had to divide the chips into bags, seal them, and stick on labels.

And finish our homework.

I held out my hands to Irv. "Chips, please."

Irv brought them out. I let out a cry of joy. Our chips looked and smelled *so* good.

Then he pointed Jaye to the stack of the recipe cards on the counter next to his laptop. "You know what to do."

Jaye flexed her fingers. And started to type.

"Go, go, go!" I cheered as Jaye finished the first one. "You're typing at warp speed."

Irv watched. "Yeah, she's fast."

Then he placed a plate of warm sugar cookies in front of us.

Jaye stopped typing and sniffed. "Yum."

I pushed the cookies away and glared at Irv. "Is this a trick to slow her down?"

He snorted. "Aren't you prickly?"

"Me? What about you?"

Meanwhile, Jaye had snatched a cookie. She typed with her right hand and ate with her left. Even though I tried to resist, I ended up eating two.

For a mean guy, he made good cookies.

"So Henry got punished way worse than I did," I told Jaye as she typed. "My parents said he was supposed to set an example, because he's older. I just have to clean out the garage. And now Henry thinks I owe him crickets to feed his lizard. Can you believe it?"

"Shh!" Irv pointed to me. "Rule one: no making noise."

"Fine." I pulled out the labels we'd printed. The label for the front of the bag had our logo.

The label for the back said:

Made in a home kitchen with ♥ for the planet!
Ingredients (all organic): corn masa, cricket powder, vegetable oil, seasonings
1 CRICKET PER CHIP!
NO gluten, nuts, or dairy
delicious FLAVOR & outrageous CRUNCH!

"Here." Irv came over and slid a box across the counter. "Free bags for your chips."

"Thanks"—I pushed them back—"but we can't use these. They're plastic."

"So?"

"So Chirps is about sustainability. Our packaging needs to be recyclable and biodegradable," I explained. "We're trying to reduce the carbon footprint on Earth."

"Oh, come on," Irv scoffed. "Just use 'em. These bags are one less thing to pay for. Didn't I hear you say you had no money?"

"We can't." I explained how humans were trashing the planet with all the plastic that ended up in landfills.

"Listen up. I once ran a business. Umbrellas. I sold umbrellas, so I know something." Irv leaned forward. "It's good you want to be responsible. But if you don't make money, you go out of business."

"I know that."

"You're going to have to pay for special paper bags. That means adding to the cost of your product. You'll need to ask people to fork over *more* money for your snack to make a profit. All because you want to save the planet?"

"Shouldn't a healthy, livable planet be worth paying a little more?" I shot back.

"*Hmmpf!*" Irv shoved his box of plastic bags into a cabinet.

Jaye and I had already talked this out. We'd used plastic baggies when we first started, but paper definitely made more sense for Chirps going forward. I pulled out the brown lunch bags I'd swiped from home. "These will work for now, and they're free, too."

"They're awfully large." Irv sounded exasperated.

He was right. But I wasn't going to agree with him.

"Have you ever opened a bag of potato chips? There's tons of air inside," I pointed out. "More air than chips."

I thought I saw him grin, but it was hard to be sure.

Mari helped me stick the labels on the bags.

Jaye typed.

Irv muttered about having ordered way too many ingredients for his Tex-Mex cooking class. He didn't know what to do with them all.

Jaye typed.

Mari and I scooped the chips into the bags.

Jaye typed.

We sealed the bags with a heart sticker.

Jaye typed.

"Done!" she finally cried.

We had sixty bags of chips, ready to sell. We were back in business!

"Whoa, where do you think you're going?" Irv called, as we headed for the door. "My recipes don't look finished. Where's the borders? The spiffy design?"

"That wasn't part of the deal," Jaye protested.

"I recall it was," Irv said. "You'll have to come back again."

I clutched the chip bags to my chest as they debated this. This time he'd have to tear our chips out of my hands.

"A piece of business advice. Free of charge. Put all deals in writing." Irv tapped his fingers on the counter. "So you'll come back?"

"B-b-but . . ." Jaye sputtered.

I pulled her to the side of the room. "He's trying to trick

us. I say we make a run for it." I eyed the door. "We have our chips. On the count of three."

"You know, it wouldn't be the worst thing, coming back," Jaye whispered. "You have to admit this setup is sweet. And we need to bake a lot more chips."

"No way." I shook my head. "He's cranky. And he's always arguing. We don't need him."

"He's not so bad."

I rolled my eyes.

"Okay, fine, but his kitchen is great. And we need that," she pointed out.

Even though I wasn't for it, Jaye went to Irv to make a new deal.

I opened my Listbook. This time I was writing everything down!

Chirps founders (Jaye & Hallie) and Irv Nellis agree that:

Chirps founders will COMPLETELY design Irv's cookbook (until he is happy with it) in exchange for UNLIMITED use of rec center kitchen, including baking supplies and spices. (Clean up and not talking rules still apply.)

Jaye Wu
_____

Hallie Amberose
_____

Irv Nellis
_____

Mari Nellis
guarantor/witness

CHAPTER 13
JAYE

Hallie and I wore our matching EAT BUGS T-shirts to the bake sale Wednesday night. Marika drove us to school after dinner, and the first thing I did was scan the lobby for Spencer. I spotted his mom organizing everyone, but I didn't see him anywhere.

I exhaled. I hadn't told Hallie the bake sale was his idea. I knew she'd think Spencer was trying to sabotage us. He did that once, and I didn't feel like defending him. Did playing basketball in his driveway mean we were friends again? I wasn't sure. But this morning we hadn't waited for the bus together in icy silence like we had all month. Just regular silence. So that was a start.

Hallie and I got to work setting up.

We covered a small table with a green-and-purple tie-dyed tablecloth.

We placed the paper bags of chips in two wicker baskets beside the table.

Hallie stood on a chair to tape our new sign onto the wall.

I blew up green and purple balloons.

Then I had an amazing idea. Mr. Thompson had told us it was important to have a lot of signage. Why not use balloons? I took a black marker and wrote EAT BUGS on a balloon.

I started to blow it up.

The more air I added, the bigger the words grew.

EAT BUGS

EAT BUGS

EAT BUGS

I wanted to see how big it could go.

EAT BUGS
EAT BUGS

As the balloon exploded like a firecracker, Hallie cried out in surprise—and stumbled off the chair.

Crunch! Her foot landed smack in the middle of one of the wicker baskets.

Breaking our chips to bits.

CHAPTER 14
HALLIE

Everything we'd been working for was in pieces.

"I'm sorry." I stared at the bags crushed under my high-top sneaker. "I got scared."

"No, it was me," Jaye said.

I stepped back to see how bad it was. Sixteen bags of chips lost. I chewed my bottom lip.

"It's my fault. It's all my fault," Jaye kept repeating. She started pacing.

Parents had begun crowding the school hallway for the

bake sale. I needed her to stop freaking out.

I took a deep breath and put my hands on her shoulders. "Listen, this is our big chance. We need to stay positive. Smile."

Mr. T said happy people are better sales people.

Happy Hallie—that's me.

Mr. T's Secrets to Selling

1. Greet with a SMILE.

2. Make EYE CONTACT when you talk.

EYE CONTACT

3. Tell a TRUE story about your product.

4. Be ENTHUSIASTIC!

5. Give a great reason WHY to buy.

6. Make the sale.

I quickly placed the forty-four bags of unbroken chips on top of the table.

"I'll go throw the broken ones away," Jaye offered.

"Later." I shoved them under the table. Then I started greeting everyone who walked by. "Hi, there! Want to buy cricket chips? They're healthier than a cupcake—and just as delicious."

"Healthier how?" one woman asked.

I told her about the protein, low carbs, and natural ingredients.

"Can you taste the bugs?" one man asked.

Not at all, I explained.

"They look like regular chips," said a boy.

I pointed out they were much better than regular chips. They had crickets in them. I mean, what beats that?

People were curious. They asked a lot of questions. Jaye and I told stories. We gave good answers. And then . . . they walked away.

Without buying chips.

"Maybe they didn't bring money?" Jaye suggested, after this happened three times.

But later we saw those same folks chowing down on brownies or cookies.

They had money. Just not for our chips.

"The Eat Bugs girls!" Mr. T boomed as he came over. He had on a suit and tie, which he never wore in the classroom. "I'm digging the whole look here. Are you racking up sales?"

"Hardly," said Jaye.

"Something's not working." I filled him in.

He clapped his hands together. "You need to give out puppies."

I looked at Jaye. She looked at me. *Puppies?* Where were we going to get puppies?

"Not literal puppies. Think of it like this. You go into a pet store and see a cute puppy. The salesperson, if she's smart, immediately scoops it up and lets you hold it. Once that adorable bundle of fur snuggles in your arms, there's a very high chance you're bringing the pup home."

"So"—I was trying to understand Mr. T—"we should let people try our chips?"

"Exactly. Free samples are a great sales tool."

"We don't really have any extras," Jaye said.

"Yes, we do." I pulled the basket out from under the table. "Ta-da!"

"They're crushed." Jaye pushed them away.

"No, they're not." I grinned. "Now, they're *bite*-size."

"That's what I'm talking about." Mr. T gave me a fist bump.

"I have another idea." Jaye raced off and returned with three bags of tortilla chips from the cafeteria vending machine. She'd also borrowed two big bowls from Spencer's mom.

She dumped our cracked cricket chips into one bowl.

She dropped the bags of regular chips on the floor.

Bam! She jumped on them.

Then she poured those broken chips into the other bowl.

She placed both bowls side-by-side and made a sign:

TASTE TEST

Can you choose the chip made with **?**

I found my mom talking with one of Henry's old teachers and borrowed the floral scarf she'd tied in her hair. We had to hurry. The bake sale would soon be over. It was truly go-big-or-go-home time.

I stood on the chair. In my loudest voice, I called, "Test your taste buds! Can you pick the chip with the cricket in it?"

A bunch of curious parents lined up. One by one, they tied on the scarf blindfold and made a guess. Some were right. Some were wrong. That didn't matter. A crowd had gathered. Everyone wanted a turn.

And a bag of chips. Or two.

We sold all forty-four bags—and the three bags we'd had left over from the park.

Mr. T gave us fist bumps. Mom hugged us.

Chirps was a success!

Woo-hoo! I knew it would be. The dream team couldn't fail!

# bags sold	to who	where
17	families and soccer players	Brookdale Park
47	parents	PTA bake sale
64/200		

CHAPTER 15
JAYE

"We did it!" I called as I opened my front door. Kicking off my sneakers, I hurried into the kitchen to tell everyone about selling the chips.

"Shhh!" Mama sat alone at the table, studying a screen on her computer. The rest of the house was dark. "Baba went upstairs to make sure Eddie goes to sleep."

"But it's only seven-thirty."

"It is important he is rested. Remember, Jie? Tomorrow is the qualifying tournament. He must win to be eligible for the big tournament. Nai Nai has gone to bed, too."

I told her about the bake sale. Mama half-listened. Her attention was on the tennis rules on the computer.

Eddie . . . again . . .

So I went to my bedroom.

I folded a lion. And three dragons.

Then I texted Ava. She was watching a show I'd never seen. She tried to tell me the plot, but I couldn't keep track of all the characters.

I texted Jazmina. She was eating one of Bryar's fancy chocolate muffins. Her mom was friends with Bryar's mom, and Bryar had gone to the moms' book club and sold them there. Jazmina said Bryar was going to Lily's party, too.

It seemed like Lily had invited everyone. Except Hallie.

I folded a swan.

Then I texted Hallie.

what r u doing?

helping henry give randall a bath

lizards take baths????

yep & I made him an itty-bitty towel!

lol—I wanna see!!!!

Friday? a sleepover—you + me!

I stopped texting. Friday night was Lily's party. I couldn't not go.

can't. family thing.

:'(is it for eddie's tennis?

That wasn't true. But it could've been. Everything these days was for Eddie. Even so, it hurt to lie to Hallie.

> good nite . . . don't let the bedbugs

> bite . . .

> or the crickets cry . . .

> or the wasps weep . . .

> or the beetles bawl . . .

We went on like this until we ran out of bugs.

Before I crawled into bed, I folded a little origami

tennis racquet and slipped it under Eddie's door. For luck.

I covered my yawn as Hallie and I waited our turn on Saturday afternoon. All the pitch teams had returned to Hotel Tremain for a mandatory check-in session with Mr. Fletcher.

The two hot sauce boys found us right away. They showed us the hot sauce challenge video they'd posted to social media. They'd already sold two hundred bottles.

"We're almost done, too," Hallie boasted.

Her math was off. Sixty-four bags wasn't even half done. But they didn't need to know that.

"So Eddie won, right? What's next for the little dude?" Hallie asked after we shook the hot sauce boys off.

"The big Turkey Trot Tournament at the town tennis center."

"And turkeys have what to do with tennis?"

"Nothing. The tournament starts Thanksgiving week."

"Gotcha. So did your family celebrate big time? What did Nai Nai cook?"

Hallie loved my grandma's food. I told her about the crescent-shaped jiaozi, salt-and-pepper shrimp, and nián gāo, sticky rice cakes. Nai Nai usually only made us nián gāo to celebrate the Lunar New Year, but she said all these foods would bring Eddie continued good luck. Throughout dinner, his shiny trophy sat triumphantly in the middle of the table.

The longer I stared at it, the more I wanted a special dinner, too. Not my usual get-an-A-on-a-test ice cream but a full-out winner celebration.

The pitch competition was my chance. One thousand dollars and a trip to New York City was way more impressive than a tennis trophy.

"Make room." Raul and Peter slipped into line behind us. They were talking about their innovative marketing idea.

We'd started brainstorming ours, but hadn't landed on anything "wow." Our best idea was drawing a cricket with color chalk on every sidewalk in town.

This is how I draw a cricket

And this is how Hallie draws one

So, yeah, we needed a better idea.

"We're having a contest in my mom's newspaper for the Summer Sled," Peter told me. His mom edited the local paper. "Little kids write in the one winter thing they wish they could do all year round."

"Like Christmas. Or skiing," Raul put in. "The winner gets a free sled. Ka-boom!"

"That's awesome," I said.

"Who judges? Is it best art or best idea that wins? What kind of drawing?" Hallie peppered them with questions.

"Details, schmetails." Peter waved her off. "We're *branding* here. Getting our name in front of everyone. That's the trick."

Raul turned away from Hallie to face me. "Spencer told me he gave you that boss bake sale idea. My dad was there and did your taste test thingy. He even bought a bag of your chips, which was stupid 'cause you'd just give me some."

"Nope, you've got to buy them like everyone else. Making money. *That's* the trick." I grinned at Peter.

"Wait, did he say *Spencer's* idea?" Hallie widened her eyes.

"Yeah." I pulled on a strand of my hair. "You see, I was hanging out at his house and . . ."

"Hey, Jaye." Posie suddenly appeared beside me. "I have to know. Did you get that sweater you wore last night from Sparks?"

I did, but normally I don't ever get to shop there 'cause everything costs way too much. But for my birthday this summer, Spencer—well, it was probably his mom who chose it—gave me a gift card.

I nodded to Posie, then widened my eyes to signal to stop talking about last night.

"That's what Erica guessed." Posie didn't clue into my message. "It was fun, being back with you guys. I'm glad Lily invited me to her party."

Hallie gave a jagged inhale and turned to stare at me. My heart began thumping rapidly.

I cringed. I had wanted to keep it secret, but I should've realized someone would talk about the party.

"H-how's your hospital kit?" My attempt to change the conversation was lame.

"Wow, I'm wiped," Posie yawned. "We stayed up so late. And all that pizza! Lily's house has a kind of funny smell, don't you think?"

"Hey, yeah, I smelled it, too," Raul chimed in.

"Kind of like my dog after she has a bath," Peter agreed.

"Jaye? You went to Lily's party *last night*?" Hallie sounded confused.

My cheeks grew warm. Embarrassed, I shifted my gaze to the rose-colored carpet, unable to meet her eyes. My mind raced for the right thing to say. "I'm sorry. I should've—"

At that moment, Mr. Fletcher called us forward, cutting off my weak apology. He asked for an update.

I showed him our sales chart. I told him the money we'd made at the bake sale went to the PTA and not back into the business. I explained how we'd bartered with Irv. And about the cricket hotel fail.

Hallie said nothing. Total silence, which was supremely weird for her. I kept stealing glances her way, but she wouldn't catch my eye.

Mr. Fletcher rubbed his hand over his bald head. "Seems like you can use a bit of help. How about I modify the challenge? You only need to sell one hundred bags. That'll give you time to work on your innovative idea and your pitch."

His offer got Hallie speaking. "Are other teams doing this?"

"Well, no," he admitted.

"Then we're not," she declared.

She hadn't asked me, but I agreed. We wanted to win—but without special treatment.

"Okay, then, what about buying ready-made cricket powder? It would make the process easier."

"I researched that already," Hallie said. "It costs way more than buying crickets and making the powder ourselves.

We don't have the money."

"*Now*," I added. "If we win, we'll use the prize money to buy cricket powder."

"Maybe." Hallie shut me down.

Mr. Fletcher pushed his fingertips together. "So, then, you need crickets."

"Yep, but I'm really picky about the crickets we use," Hallie explained. "I want to know what they ate. Where they slept. The music they listened to."

"The music?" He grinned. "Ah, so homegrown and happy?"

"Exactly!" Hallie leaned forward, as if they were the only two in the room. "Not any ol' mail-order crickets. People should know everything about what they eat. Like a chicken nugget—what is that, really? Do you know?"

They talked about food, but I'd stopped listening. I had messed up. Badly. I saw that now. I wished Hallie hadn't heard I went to the party from Posie and Raul.

"I have a lead for you," Mr. Fletcher declared, bringing me back to the meeting. He scrolled through his phone. "Dipti Bakshi is a friend of a friend. I hear she has some sort of bug farm about thirty minutes away."

Hallie wrote the web address and phone number in her Listbook.

"Thanks." Hallie beamed at him. She kept ignoring me.

Mr. Fletcher paused, studying us. "Everything okay here? I'm sensing tension."

"We're fine," I said quickly. Hallie said nothing.

"Look, I'm going to be straight with you. You're definitely way behind the other teams." He rubbed his palms together. "If you hit the accelerator now, you can get back on the road. But you need to be in the car *together*. Understand? Did you know that sixty-two percent of all startups fail because of conflicts between the founders?"

I gulped. I didn't want us to fail. I didn't want Hallie mad at me.

"We're good," I assured him as Raul and Peter stepped forward for their turn.

As soon as Hallie and I were out of earshot, I started to apologize.

But she had already stormed away.

CHAPTER 16
HALLIE

I flopped onto an oversize daybed in the center of the hotel lobby. Lying on my back, I stared up at the brass chandelier. Tears pooled in the corner of my eyes. I tried to blink them away.

I felt so stupid.

Jaye lied to me. She told me she couldn't come for a sleepover, but the real reason was the party. She'd gone back to them. Just like I knew she would.

Because they were popular.

A moment later, Jaye ran over. "I can explain."

"You lied." I studied my fingers. "Twice. Maybe more."

"I didn't mean to." She sat on the edge of the daybed. "It's complicated."

"Being friends with me, you mean."

"What? No. I didn't want you to be sad about the party. That's why I didn't tell you."

"I don't care about the party. Lily's a fake. They all are." I refused to look at her.

"That's harsh. They aren't. You'd know that if you got to know them," she said.

"I know them enough," I shot back. "If you want to do sleepovers with them and not me, just tell me. Don't pretend you have something else to do, like a dinner for Eddie."

"That's not it."

"Oh, come on. You just told me what Nai Nai cooked last night!"

"We did have the dinner. Just on Thursday night, not last night." Jaye kicked at the carpet with the toe of her sneaker. "I'm sorry. I wanted you to think that Lily hadn't invited me, either."

"You don't need to pretend to be unpopular for me."

"I'm not popular."

"You are." Jaye didn't see how much everyone liked her. Especially now that she'd finally stepped out of Spencer and Erica's shadow. They thought I was weird. They've always thought that. "And Spencer? You guys best buds again?" I couldn't hide my jealousy.

"Not really."

"I think he's mean." I wondered if they talked about me. Laughed about me.

"That's why I didn't say anything. I didn't want to upset you."

"Well, you did."

"I'm sorry."

"Look, we should just be business partners." I worked to keep my voice steady. "We don't need to do friend stuff, sleepovers and that kind of thing."

"But I want to be your friend."

"And be friends with them?" I grimaced.

Jaye leaned back so her head rested next to mine. "Yes. Why not?" She sighed deeply. "I wish everyone I'm friends with was friends with each other."

"Not happening." I told Jaye I didn't want to hang with Spencer and Erica—even if she did. They'd never been nice to me. "I thought you and I were a team. The Super Slayers."

"We are." Then she added quietly. "It can't always be just us."

I didn't understand why not.

"I like being friends with lots of people," Jaye continued.

Stung, I examined the chipped turquoise polish on my fingernails. I didn't know what that meant for me.

"Okay, no Spencer for you. Fine," Jaye said. "But what about Ava, Sophia, and Jazmina? You like them, right?"

"Yeah, they're okay." That was true. They'd never said anything mean. At least, nothing I'd heard. But I didn't really know them much. "Do they like me?"

"Totally. But you should talk to them at lunch. You talk just to me. About Chirps mostly," she pointed out.

"I do not."

"You do." She gave me a nudge. "Come on, Hals. You're always chatting up random people at the rec center. Why do you ignore them?"

I wrapped my arms around myself. The truth was I was scared to say the wrong thing. Scared they'd turn Jaye against me. "I'm not really a group-friend person."

Her shoulders slumped, and that's when I saw how

much she wanted all her friends to be friends.

"I'll try. I promise," I told her. I meant it, too. "But Chirps . . . it's just us, right?"

"Definitely. We're in a car driving somewhere, didn't you hear?" Jaye joked.

"I did." I smiled back.

"Please don't be mad about what I did." Jaye put her hands together.

"I'm not." I wasn't good at staying angry anyway. "But from now on, tell the truth. I can take it."

We lay there, staring at the ceiling. I listened to the wheels of suitcases rolling across the lobby floor. The ring of a cell phone. Someone talking about nearby restaurants.

"I didn't stay for the sleepover part. Nai Nai picked me up," Jaye said suddenly.

I twisted to see her face. "Was the party bad?"

"No. I pretended to Lily that Eddie had an early morning match I had to wake up for." Her voice quivered. "I can't have sleepovers. Ever. With anyone. Even you. I make up an excuse whenever I'm asked."

I thought back on all the times I'd asked her to sleep over.

"Are you afraid of the dark? I was for, like, years."

"No. My parents, and Nai Nai, too, they won't let me. They say I have a perfectly good bed at home." She propped herself up. "They never had sleepovers when they were kids. They don't get it."

"Well, I've only slept at Zara's house and my two cousins' houses. You're not missing much." I sat up and whispered in her ear. "Besides, I've heard Lily's house smells like wet dog."

Jaye laughed. "It did."

She reached into the back pocket of her jeans and handed me an origami giraffe.

I marveled at all the intricate folds. "So cool."

"You think?" Jaye hesitated then said. "No one knows about my paper animals, either."

"I think they're awesome. Can I keep it?"

Jaye nodded, and I tucked the giraffe safely inside my Listbook.

We were okay again. Chirps wasn't going to fail because of cofounder conflict.

Chirps wasn't going to fail. Period.

I pointed to Dipti's name. "Want to go visit a real cricket farm?"

CHAPTER 17
JAYE

"This doesn't look like a farm. Where's the barn?" I stared at an enormous, ancient brick building. It had rusted iron-framed windows and cracked concrete steps.

We were a few blocks off the highway. Except for a gas station and laundromat at the far end of the street, the nearby stores were mostly vacant. Some were boarded up.

"Cricket farms aren't like Old MacDonald farms," Hallie told me.

"It's an old warehouse." Hallie's dad explained.

"This place is creepy." I shivered as Hallie led us to the front door. A small metal plate read BAKSHI BUG FARM.

We'd tried calling Dipti before we left the hotel, but it went to voicemail. When Mr. Amberose picked us up, we'd pleaded with him to drive out here, anyway. With only fourteen days to go, we couldn't waste one more minute.

He rang the bell.

"Who's there?" a female voice crackled over an intercom.

Hallie announced us. "We came to see the bug farm."

The door buzzed open. I flipped up the hood of my blue parka and took a deep breath, ready to battle the cobwebs and dust. I was sure this place would be gross.

We stepped inside—and were instantly surrounded by a hurricane of sound. Chirping! So much chirping!

I gazed about in wonder.

The walls were painted bright white. Rows of white tubs with identical clipboard charts lined the perimeter of the room. Shiny chrome lights glowed over each bin.

It looked more like my parents' science lab than a run-down warehouse.

A young woman with dark hair twisted into a messy bun hurried over. She wore a white lab coat, latex gloves, and faded jeans. As soon as we told her Mr. Fletcher had sent us, she introduced herself as Dipti.

The creating a business part of Chirps excites me. And the saving the world part, too. The bug part is Hallie's jam. And she was in bug heaven.

Not only did Dipti have thousands of crickets (as well as lots of other types of bugs), but they were clean, cared for, and—get this—ate leftovers donated from a high-class vegetarian restaurant. She had us scrub our hands and wear gloves, then she showed us how the temperature, humidity, and air flow were monitored. The different bins held crickets at different stages of their lives. Crickets only live for twelve weeks. After they have babies, they die.

And Dipti played classical music for the babies from two portable speakers.

Seriously, if Hallie could've moved in, she would have.

The bug farm, I mean, not the cricket bins.

I stayed a step behind during the tour. Frozen solid or roasted to a crisp is how I liked my crickets. None of this creepy-crawly stuff. I was happy when Dipti circled us back to the front entryway.

"Why are you in this"—I was going to say *gross* but caught myself—"old building?"

"The beauty of raising edible insects is that they don't need fields to roam," Dipti explained. "Or streams. Or sunshine. They can be raised inside. Anywhere. Even in small spaces. Even in cities."

This made edible bug farms especially good problem solvers for developing countries with lots of people to feed, she told us. She wanted to build farms there, once she got this one up and running.

I hoped Hallie was taking notes. This was good stuff for our pitch.

"I got a really sweet deal to rent this place," Dipti explained. "All it needed was a scrubbing and fresh paint. I'm just starting out, so I don't have much money. I had to get creative."

"Think outside the box." Hallie gave me the finger-antennae wiggle. "We know all about that."

Dipti explained that her farm supplied bugs to food companies and to restaurants. But she only sold in large quantities. And her bugs were expensive. And she didn't sell directly to people walking in off the street.

Like us.

"Any chance you'd donate some crickets?" I gave her my most convincing smile.

"I'm sorry. I love what you're doing, but I'm running a small business. I've got to watch my numbers." Dipti said she'd be rooting for us.

Rooting for us? We didn't need a cheerleader, we needed bugs.

She started to say goodbye.

We couldn't leave—not yet. I tried to puzzle out an answer.

Dipti was a small business owner, just like us. She'd made a deal to get the warehouse. We'd made a deal with Irv.

Could Hallie and I make a deal with Dipti, too?

"How about we trade you for crickets?" I suggested. "I'm good at designing stuff on a computer. Like cookbooks."

"My mom's an artist. She could paint a sign for out front," Hallie offered. "Or my dad could take some photos, right Dad?"

"My brother's super good at tennis. I bet he could teach you," I threw in.

Hailey held up my origami giraffe. "Jaye makes these."

"Any animal you want, it's yours," I told her.

"Whoa!" Dipti chuckled, but she wasn't interested in a trade.

I wouldn't give up. "What if you gave us three thousand crickets now? We can't pay you today, but we promise to pay you in three months. And we'll pay *more* money then."

"That's called interest," Hallie filled in. Mr. Thompson had taught us about interest in BEE class.

"And we'll write on our labels that the crickets came from here—"

"Which is great advertising for you." Hallie finished again.

Dipti smirked. "You two are quite the tag team."

"What do you think?" I asked eagerly. "You'd really be helping us out. Like majorly."

"How do I know you'll pay me later?" She narrowed her dark eyes. "Maybe you give me something to hold onto. Something important to you."

I chewed the inside of my cheek, trying to think of something valuable I owned that she'd want.

"I'll cover them." Hailey's dad stepped up. "If they can't pay, I will. Beats crickets in my bed any day." He ruffled Hallie's hair.

"We'll pay," I assured Dipti and Mr. Amberose.

"Come on, don't you want to help a bunch of cute kids?" Hallie pleaded with Dipti. "We really need it."

The crickets seemed to go silent, as we all waited for her answer.

"Yeesh." She threw up her hands. "Okay, we have a deal. I'll be your first supplier."

We added another agreement to Hallie's Listbook.

I never thought I'd be so happy to own three thousand crickets.

Bakshi Bug Farm (Dipti) agrees to give Chirps (Jaye & Hallie)

3,000 crickets today, and Chirps will pay BBF $200 ($180 + $20 interest) by February 20.

BBF to be listed on bag label (and Hallie and Jaye will be FOREVER grateful).

Jaye Wu

Hallie Amberose

Dipti Bakshi

Stan Amberose
guarantor/witness

CHAPTER 18
HALLIE

"If your heart is in your dream,
no request is too extreme."
—the very wise Jiminy Cricket

There was total silence as the neon-yellow ball whizzed low and hard across the net. Eddie sprang into action, his quick feet landing him in front of the ball just in time. He punched the volley deep, out of reach of his opponent. Another winner!

The little dude was blowing my mind.

"Woo-hooo!" I screamed.

Jaye tugged my arm to get me to sit. She'd warned me

that tennis fans don't cheer wildly. But how could I not?
Eddie was wiping the court with the other kid.

I'd invited myself to join Jaye's family at the tennis
center on Monday afternoon. I'd wanted to see what it was
all about.

And of course, I dressed for it. White visor. My hair pulled into a high ponytail. White sweater. Retro terry sweatbands on both wrists. I wished I owned a tennis dress.

I looked around. The stands were nearly filled. "Why are so many people here to watch little kids?"

"It's not only Eddie's age," Jaye's mom said. "All different ages. People stay and watch many matches."

Nai Nai nodded. "On the day of the finals, it will be very hard to find a seat."

And that got me thinking.

"Here's another stupendous idea," I announced. "If Eddie makes it to the finals, we have him wear the cricket costume while he plays."

"The green one with the bulging eyes?" Jaye sounded shocked. "You want him to play in that?"

"Definitely." I'd worn it for our school pitch competition. "It'll get everyone talking about Chirps."

Nai Nai chuckled. "Hallie, you're too funny."

But I wasn't joking. It was perfect for the innovative part of the pitch challenge. People would post about a huge cricket playing tennis. And they'd mention Chirps. It would go viral then *wham!*—everyone would want to try our chips.

"I'll decorate Eddie's tennis racquet to look like a fly swatter!" I nudged Jaye. "Tell me that's not genius?"

"It will get him disqualified," Jaye said.

"*Shhh.* Eddie's serving," Jaye's mom hushed us.

We all went quiet and watched Eddie. He won easily. I had no doubt he'd make it to the finals.

Now all I had to do was figure out how to get a massive cricket on the court.

Now more than ever, I wanted to win the pitch competition. The prize money would let us build Chirps. But there was another reason. Without the prize money, I wasn't sure if Chirps would survive. And as long as there was Chirps, there was me and Jaye.

If Eddie couldn't wear the costume, I would.

CHAPTER 19
JAYE

"Hallie wants my brother to dress like a cricket," I told Mari on Tuesday afternoon.

It was never happening, of course. My family didn't do things like that.

"In a costume?" Mari looked up eagerly. She'd been playing with a bunch of origami animals I'd fished from the pockets of my backpack. Some were crumpled, but she didn't seem to care.

I was designing Irv's recipes as fast as I could. Borders.

Cool fonts. Colors. I planned to be done before Hallie's mom dropped her off after her dentist appointment.

We still had three thousand crickets to roast.

"Nana had lots of costumes," Mari told me. "We were both mermaids. Can you fold me a mermaid?"

"You remember that?" Irv stopped mumbling about not knowing what to cook with all his extra cheese and salsa.

"Nana was a space princess. And a ladybug."

"You're right." He came to sit by Mari. "Your nana sure loved dressing up."

Then he turned to me. "Millie worked at Kostume Kart. Each day in October, she wore a different costume leading up to Halloween. She'd wear them to the grocery store, the coffee place, anywhere. Millie always said life was more fun in costume."

Irv smiled at the memory but sounded sad. Nai Nai had his same happy-sad expression whenever she told stories about my grandfather. He died when I was Mari's age.

"Did you dress up, too?" I asked.

"Irv? Dress up? Honey, you're talking to Mr. Grumps." Deanna appeared in the doorway. She'd stopped in to grab a roll of paper towels.

"For your information, I wasn't grumpy with Millie," Irv shot back.

"I know." Deanna stopped teasing him. "You two were lovely together."

I could tell Irv missed her a lot. "How did you two meet?"

I loved meet-cute stories. I always made Nai Nai tell the story of how she and Ye Ye met at a bus stop when she got on the wrong bus.

"We were counselors at a summer camp in the Poconos. I was in charge of the waterfront. She was the drama counselor. One hot day, she took a canoe out during her rest hour. And, for whatever reason, she stood up. She said it was to better see the fish below. Well, she saw those fish real well"—Irv chuckled—"because she toppled in. I heard the splash and rowed out to help her."

"Did you save her?"

"Not even a little. She'd scrambled back into her boat before I'd reached her. But we floated out there in our separate boats, talking and talking."

"Show Jaye that picture," Deanna urged.

Irv opened his worn brown leather wallet and pulled own a tiny photo. Younger, thinner Irv looking swanky in a dark tuxedo. His full head of light brown hair swooped to one side. He gazed at Millie, wearing a strapless fuschia party dress with a full skirt. She was laughing, her exuberant joy bursting through the hand she held in front of her mouth.

"Millie had a lot of energy. And so many ideas." Irv ran his finger around the worn edge of the photo. "She liked to joke that she married me to anchor her. Otherwise, she said, she'd float into the sky like a helium balloon."

"She sounds like Hallie," I remarked.

"Yep, that partner of yours certainly has my Millie's

spunk." He gazed around. "Awfully quiet today without her jabbering."

I grinned. I think Irv actually missed Hallie.

At that moment, Hallie burst into the kitchen, waving a piece of paper. "Did you know about this?"

GRAND OPENING CELEBRATION!

Rec Center Gym
Join us!
demonstrations, games, face painting, prizes, fun
Tuesday, November 30th

"Yeah, that's where they're selling Irv's cookbook." I turned to him. "It's finished, by the way. Ready to print. But I'll show you how to do borders if you want to change something."

"Jaye, are you not seeing what I'm seeing?" Hallie

bounced on the toes of her Converse sneakers. "This is a legit carnival. Best place ever for a huge cricket. Way better than a tennis court. We can sell tons of chips."

We needed to do that. Mr. Thompson had pulled us aside yesterday during BEE. He didn't know if we'd sell all the chips in time. He was worried for us. And that made me worried.

Hallie had wanted to bike around the neighborhood to sell them door-to-door. But Nai Nai refused to let me do anything unsafe like that. The tennis center had a no-food policy during the tournament, so that was out. There weren't any school bake sales coming up, and the park was a no-go.

The grand opening was our best option, but . . .

"They won't let us sell our chips here," I told Hallie.

"Why not? It's not a park or a city street. We don't need a permit, right?" Hallie looked to Deanna.

"No, but you aren't an official rec center activity," Deanna said. "Jaye's right. I don't think it will be allowed."

"*Pshhh.*" Irv waved her off. "Listen, girls, take some business advice. Who you know is just as important as what you know."

"Who do we know?" Hallie asked.

"Me," Irv said proudly.

I suddenly put the pieces together. "Mari's mom is the rec center director. Irv, will you get us in?"

"Perhaps." He drummed his fingers on the table.

"Help 'em out, Irv." Deanna gave him a friendly nudge. "We both loved their chips."

"You tried our chips?" I was confused. "When?"

"Last week. Irv gave me a taste. He talks about you two *all* the time," she said.

Hallie whirled on him. "Hey, you said you wouldn't touch our chips!"

He shrugged. "Had to see what all the fuss was about."

"Hals, he *liked* them." I put my hand on her shoulder so she wouldn't go off on him. "Right, Irv?"

"I was impressed," he admitted. "You may be onto something."

Hallie's face broke into a wide smile. "Woo-hoo! Another bug-eater on board."

Irv snorted. "Hardly."

Hallie grew serious. She told him about the time crunch we were under. "If you get Ms. Mellits to let us sell our chips at this fiesta, Jaye and I will be forever grateful. We won't ask you for your help or anything ever again."

"It's not a fiesta. And, no." Irv shook his head.

Huh? And I'd just been thinking he'd tricked us into coming back not because he was mean but because he liked us being around. That Hallie reminded him of Millie. That he really was squishy inside, like Nai Nai said.

"Why not?" I asked.

"I'm saying no to doing this on your own, not to my asking Bess."

"You want to *help* us?" Hallie asked.

"I'd think you'd be begging for my help. I'm an excellent chef and an excellent salesperson." For the first time, Irv lost his permanent scowl. His pale eyes brightened. "Luckily, I'm offering both skills free of charge."

Hallie raised her eyebrows at me. I shrugged.

"You need more than a cricket costume to make noise. And you're going to need a lot more hands than yours and mine." Irv pushed up his glasses, thought for a moment, then leaned in. "Actually, maybe it *is* a fiesta. Well, almost. Here's my idea."

It was a put-all-your-crickets-in-one-egg-carton kind of idea. A huge gamble, especially since the pitch was only three days after the grand opening.

If this didn't work, we'd be left with nothing—no crickets, no chips, no more time, no chance of winning.

Hallie, of course, loved it.

Me? I was scared. But what choice did we have?

CHAPTER 20
HALLIE

Great Groups Names

- an orchestra of crickets
- an army of caterpillars
- a cloud of grasshoppers
- a whisper of moths
- a loveliness of ladybugs

I hid behind the trophy case in the school's main hallway, keeping watch on the yellow school bus in the circular driveway. The first kids of the day were streaming out. Ready to push open the front doors.

One . . . two . . .

I counted down the minutes silently.

Some seventh and eighth graders I didn't know entered. They shuffled down the side hall, out of sight. Then I spotted Raul. And Ava. And Jazmina.

Three . . . four . . .

I held my breath as they approached the sixth-grade wing.

"Who stuck a bug on my locker?"

"It's so cute!"

"They're everywhere!"

The hallway was infested with bugs!

Origami crickets were taped onto every sixth-grade locker.

Wanna guess who did that? Yep—but the origami had been Mari's idea. While we'd been brainstorming with Irv and Deanna, she played with a tiny cricket Jaye had folded. She pretended it was visiting all the other origami animals to invite them to our big event.

Hello? A cricket delivering a mysterious message? Brilliant!

All Thanksgiving weekend, Jaye had folded and folded. After her fingers turned bloody with paper cuts, my mom, dad, Henry, and I jumped in to help. Then Deanna and I wrote on each cricket:

nacho party!
rec center ✳ tuesday ✳ 4:00pm

Nothing else. No explanation.

Today, we came to school super early. Mr. T had us clear it first with Mrs. Leary, the principal. We explained that our paper crickets were just like putting up a flyer.

Only way cuter.

My phone pinged. Jaye texted a video from the other side of the school. The sixth graders there were buzzing, too.

"Hey, Bug Girl!" Raul sauntered over, a purple cricket resting on his palm. "You did this, right?"

I knew it wouldn't take kids long to put it together.

Peter joined him, holding out a blue cricket. "What's it mean?"

"Come to the rec center and you'll see." I tried to make my smile mysterious.

"Just tell us what you're up to," Raul said. "We told you about our idea."

I'd seen their Summer Sled art contest in the newspaper last week. It was definitely the kind of contest I would've entered a few years ago.

"No can do." Jaye and I had vowed to keep our lips zipped. "But the surprise will be epic."

That's what I kept saying over and over all day.

"This is lame." Raul waved the cricket in my face. Then he took off with Peter toward first period, passing the big trash bin by the office. But they didn't toss them in. Instead,

I watched each tuck the cricket into his pocket.

Saving it.

After second period, I met Jaye by the water fountain. I slipped my phone from my backpack and secretly showed her the photo Henry had sent from the high school.

He'd tacked an origami cricket onto every bulletin board!

Jaye waited for me outside Mrs. Stein's door after fourth period. We checked my phone again: a pic from Deanna. It showed the kids in her childcare room holding up origami crickets to bring home to their parents. I pulled Jaye inside the classroom, pointing to Mrs. Stein. She'd pinned the cricket I'd given her onto the collar of her cardigan.

At lunch, we huddled together in a bathroom stall. Dipti had sent a photo of her social media post, featuring our origami cricket. Others had started reposting. Spencer's mom had forwarded that same photo to the whole PTA. That was a ton of families!

That day, origami crickets appeared all over Brookdale. The counter guy at the pet food store—the place I'd bought our crickets when we first started everything—placed one on his cash register for every customer to see. Officer Costas put one on his desk in the police station. Nai Nai carried them in her big black handbag, passing them out at the market, the post office, and the drug store.

The word was spreading with the help of our cricket orchestra.

I was so pumped for the stunt we'd planned. We'd worked nonstop all week: folding paper, roasting three thousand crickets, baking chip after chip after chip.

All we needed was for people to show up. A lot of people.

Would they?

Could we actually pull this off?

CHAPTER 21
JAYE

"Pour salsa over here. Sprinkle more cheese on the edges."
I stood on a folding chair to get an aerial view. Below me,
covering an entire Ping-Pong table lined with aluminum
foil, was the biggest platter of nachos the town of Brookdale
had ever seen.

The nacho party was Irv's idea. He'd given us the extra
cheese and salsa from his cooking class. "Melt cheese on
anything and it's a winner," he'd said. "It'll get people to
check out your chips."

It was my idea to make it a *really* big platter. We'd hand out scoops for free. Just like at the bake sale.

Hallie decided to make it GINORMOUS.

"Let's break the world record for largest serving of nachos!" she'd cried.

Then we looked it up. The world-record nachos were more than eighty feet long and weighed over five thousand pounds.

No way we'd ever bake enough chips to beat that!

So we were going big . . . for Brookdale.

"Time check?" Ava called out. She, Jazmina, and Sophia slathered the remaining salsa on the chips. I couldn't believe they'd happily agreed to join Team Cricket for the day. They even wore antennae headbands I'd twisted from pipe cleaners.

"Five minutes to go." Then the doors to the rec center's new gym would be flung open. I spotted Henry carrying in the final pot of hot cheese sauce from Irv's kitchen. "Hurry!" I cried.

Everyone in the gym was scurrying about. A personal trainer chased an escaped red balloon from his booth. The activities director set up cones for a basketball free throw contest. The DJ adjusted volume levels on the sound system, while the bounce house in the corner got a final burst of air. Deanna dipped brushes in the face paints at the childcare booth. Next to us, Irv straightened his stack of cookbooks.

I looked over at Hallie. "All okay?"

"Stupendous!" She'd lined up one hundred and forty paper bags of our chips on a small table next to the nachos. She held up a bag. "And this! Score!"

I'd remembered the parade of puppets in Deanna's childcare room, all made from little paper bags. And it turned out she had a whole bunch extra. Bess said we could have them since we'd advertised the grand opening with our paper crickets.

One more deal to write in the Listbook.

Hallie stood on her tiptoes, scanning the gym. "Hey,

Jaye. Where's Nai Nai? She's never late. Is she coming?"

"Later." I explained that Eddie's semi-final match had started about an hour ago. She'd promised to stop in after.

"Photo booth's ready." Hallie's mom stepped back. She'd painted a cartoon black-and-white cow on a large piece of plywood, just like we'd asked. Instead of giving the cow a face, she'd cut an oval hole.

Save a Cow.
Eat a Cricket.

Ava poked her face through the hole. "Moo!"

Jazmina raised her phone. "Do cow eyes."

Ava batted her eyelashes, and Jazmina snapped a pic.

"*Udder*ly amazing," I cried.

Hallie didn't miss a beat. "Legen-*dairy!*"

"I got the *moo*-ves!" Ava joined our puns, wiggling her arms.

Hallie smiled at Jazmina, Ava, and Sophia. "*Moo*-chas *grass*-ias, you guys."

They all laughed at that one.

At the front of the gym, Bess shook a tambourine to get everyone's attention. The mayor stood beside her. Mari sat cross-legged by her feet, dressed adorably in Hallie's cricket costume. She waved at Hallie, and Hallie pointed to the sign by the nachos. She'd used a photo of Mari wearing her antennae headband and made her our official mascot.

"I declare the renovated Brookdale Rec Center officially open!" Bess reached for an enormous pair of scissors and cut the big red ribbon hanging across the double doors.

In a flash, the doors were flung wide and kids raced to the cotton candy machine. Lines formed for face painting and balloon animals. The bounce house started shaking. On the mats, tumblers showed off skills they'd learned. I spotted Spencer, Erica, Samara, Owen, and a big group of kids from school by the spin art. The origami crickets had worked!

We waited in the far corner of the gym, holding large spoons and mini paper plates, ready to dish out the steaming nachos made with our chips. We'd gone back to Dipti for more crickets to make them all.

But no one came over.

Had they not noticed us? Or did they not want any?

I shot Irv a worried look.

"Make noise," he said.

"What about rule one?" Hallie teased.

She climbed onto the chair beside me, grasping onto my shirt so we both wouldn't tumble. Cupping her hand around her mouth, she yelled, "Nachos!"

But her voice disappeared over the pounding bass of the music.

"Go again," I said to Hallie.

I slipped two fingers in my mouth and whistled the way Spencer showed me years ago.

"FREE NACHOS!" she cried, her voice filling a pause

between tunes. "FREE NACHOS!"

That did it. From that moment on, we had a steady stream of curious customers. Ava, Jazmina, Sophia, and Henry dished out nachos. And Irv was right. People who were hesitant about edible bugs gave our chips a try once they were loaded down with gooey cheese.

And lots bought a bag.

Hallie ran the photo booth. Mari, our cricket mascot, buzzed about. I sat at the table, taking money and recording our sales. We were getting closer and closer to two hundred.

With every bag sold, we handed people a round, neon-green sticker to wear. It said:

We wanted the gym to be swarming with green stickers, so that everyone would see them and get curious.

"Is this your recipe?" A woman with dark curls and huge gold hoop earrings tapped Hallie's shoulder just as we were running low on nachos. She held out Irv's cookbook.

"Ours? No. The recipes are his." Hallie pointed to Irv, sitting at his table with his arms folded behind his head.

"He said this one came from you." She opened to the final page.

I held my breath, as Hallie's mouth dropped open. I'd been waiting all afternoon for her to see it. "Surprise!" I cried.

"You didn't!" She let out an ear-piercing squeal.

I nodded. Irv had given me the okay to slip one more recipe into the book. Nachos made with cricket chips, of course!

"Irv told me to come over and talk with you." The woman was examining a bag of our chips. She reached into the pocket of her flannel coat and handed me a business card.

I sucked in my breath. She had a natural food store. And she asked us about maybe selling our chips there!

She said we'd need to change the packaging. And the amount of chips in each bag. Some other stuff too. Anything she wanted, I promised we could do it.

She told us to call her this weekend. To see if there was something we could work out.

The whole time Hallie jiggled her legs, unable to stand still. She waited until the woman walked clear across the gym to start jumping. "We did it! We're going to be in a store!"

"Only maybe," I reminded her.

"Yes. It's going to be a yes. It's the dream!" She grabbed my hand, bouncing me up and down with her.

"It's a certifiable success!" Hallie's mom joined us, the three of us in a circle. "Look at the Ping-Pong table."

There were barely any nachos left, just smears of salsa and cheese.

"Jie, don't leave that money out. Someone will take it. Put it in the envelope." Nai Nai appeared suddenly, scolding me, shaking her head at the stack of bills on the table.

I scrambled to collect it, then spotted Eddie beside her. And burst out laughing. "What are you? An intergalactic fairy?"

Eddie pouted and crossed his arms. "I'm a cricket."

He wore an old pair of my dad's lab goggles that had been painted green, and a green wool winter hat with a pom-pom on top. Angel wings I'd once used for a Halloween costume had also been painted green and now rested crookedly on his back. He wore his navy tennis warm-ups and white sneakers.

"You're awesome!" Hallie hugged Eddie.

"You said he should dress as a cricket," Nai Nai told Hallie.

"To help you win," Eddie added. "But you already have one." He pointed to Mari.

"The more the merrier, right, Jaye?" Hallie said. "That's our new thing. We so need you, little dude."

I flicked his pom-pom with my fingers. "Thanks."

He reached into the pocket of his warm-up pants and handed me an origami cricket. It was the red one I'd tucked into his tennis bag this morning. "Nai Nai said crickets bring luck." He twisted his mouth. "But yours didn't work."

"Wait, what?" I cried. "You didn't win?"

Eddie shook his head, fighting back tears.

"What happened?" I was shocked. Eddie had been seeded #1.

"Some freaky good ten-year-old with a killer serve and a dumb drop shot." Eddie pouted. "He's going to the finals. Not me."

"Bummer, little dude." Hallie straightened his crooked wings.

"Everyone there was very surprised," Nai Nai added.

"I'm sorry, Eddie." I felt a tug of sadness for my brother. It stinks not to win. It stinks even more when everyone expects you to win.

No one expected me and Hallie to win, so I guessed that was good. Mr. Fletcher didn't even think we were on the right road to win.

"Well, we're glad you're here," I told Eddie "'cause we need all the cricket power we can get."

Hallie grabbed Mari and Eddie and started dancing. She made up a bug line dance. Flapping wings. Antennae fingers. A spin with a buzz. I smiled when Jazmina and Ava joined them. Maybe, in time, all my friends would become friends. Hallie was fun, once you got to know her.

"You have worked very hard," Nai Nai whispered softly in my ear.

My grandma didn't dance or exclaim like Hallie's mom did. For Nai Nai, this was a full-out parade of praise. My body flooded with warmth.

"Everyone's talking about edible bugs," Bess declared, coming over to collect Mari as the gym emptied out. She turned to Irv. "I'm thinking we offer a special class. Cooking with bugs. Hallie and Jaye can help you teach it. What do you say, girls?"

"We could do that, but . . ." Hallie drummed her fingers on the table, mimicking Irv. "We have a lot of rules."

"Uh-uh. My kitchen, my rules," Irv crossed his arms.

"We'll see about that." Hallie crossed her arms, too, staring him down.

Then they both grinned.

I filled Irv in about the natural food store. "We may be baking more chips. What do you say? Another deal?"

"I could do that." He shook my hand, very official-like.

Then he looked over at our little table. "So? Success?

I counted up the bags. Forty-three left. I quickly did the math.

We'd sold ninety-seven bags today.

It was a lot.

But it wasn't enough.

# bags sold	to who	where
17	families and soccer players	Brookdale Park
47	parents	PTA bake sale
97	families and kids	rec center grand opening
161/200		

CHAPTER 22
HALLIE

Lucky Bug List

 Ladybugs—if one lands on you =
big money

 Dragonflies—if one lands on you =
big life change

 Bees—if one lands on your head =
big success

 Crickets—cricket in your kitchen =
good luck

"We're in so much trouble," Jaye whispered to me.

"Stop saying that." I watched the team on the stage at the front of the hotel ballroom finish up their pitch. "We're staying positive, remember?"

"I'm positive we're in trouble." Jaye moaned quietly. "My stomach hurts."

"We're ready. We know our stuff." I'd written the pitch on note cards and taped them all over my house. On the refrigerator. On the TV remote. Next to the toilet in every bathroom. Everywhere I went, there was our pitch. By now, I could recite it backward.

"Why are so many people here?" Jaye hissed. It was a blustery, gray Saturday afternoon, and the late arrivals trickled in, bundled in their coats, standing along the back and side walls. Every row of chairs in the Hotel Tremain ballroom was filled. All the pitch teams sat together in a section near the front.

"Um, the winner walks away with a thousand dollars?"

Plus there were teams from all the county middle schools. And they'd brought family and friends.

But not as many as we did.

I turned in my seat to see my mom, dad, and Henry. Jaye's whole family sat beside them—Nai Nai, Eddie, her mom, and even her dad, who I'd never met before. He wore a crisp white shirt and was studying the program in his lap with the same intensity Jaye had when she took a test. Irv had brought Mari, who wiggled her antennae headband at us, and Deanna. Mrs. Montan proudly wore a Brookdale Middle School sweatshirt. Jazmina, Ava, and Sophia, plus the rest of the Pitch Club, sat together with Mr. T. Even Mrs. Stein had come.

"Did you hear them?" Jaye nodded her chin at a boy and girl in matching navy blazers now exiting the stage. They'd created a hand sanitizer pump that attached to a front door handle. This way guests could disinfect before entering your house.

I liked it. So did the three judges sitting in the front row.

"Their product was good, but they weren't," I told Jaye. She was twisting her hair so tightly I was afraid it would tear from her scalp. "They pitched it like they were one of Henry's robots. Too stiff."

We'd bring the passion. I was sure of that.

I eyed the judges more closely. They'd been introduced at the beginning by Mr. Fletcher. Caleb Wahan, who owned a mobile dog grooming business with vans all over the state, was being the nice guy, gushing to each team how impressed he was. Darcas Reynolds, who taught business at the college, was asking the tough questions about money and plans for the future. Raul and Peter had run into problems with him, explaining why they were charging so much for their Summer Sled.

And then there was Liz Rees, the advertising agency owner who'd given the "foodies" our challenge card at the first meeting. She'd looked slightly bored and distracted the whole time. I wondered what we'd need to do to get her attention.

I jiggled my leg with anticipation, eager to get up onstage. We'd listened to over twenty pitches already: Plant watering services. Scented body lotions. Donuts for dogs. Posie had gone. And Bryar had, too. Each startup had exactly three minutes. A large digital clock on the side of the stage ticked down the time. If you ran over, you were cut off mid-pitch. This had happened to the hot sauce boys.

We'd timed ourselves over and over. We were good. If anything, we'd run short.

Finally, after what felt like forever, Mr. Fletcher announced, "Next, the founders of Chirps Chips will tell us why we should all eat bugs."

I reached under my chair for my green cricket head with the cute bulging eyes and antennae and slipped it onto my head. Costumes all the way, I say.

I gave Jaye's hand a squeeze: our Partner Power Pulse. She squeezed back. Together, me in my cricket costume and Jaye in her EAT BUGS shirt, we bounded onto the stage. The audience applauded. Looking directly at the judges, I kicked up my heels and waved.

"Hi, I'm Hallie Amberose, and this is Jaye Wu. We're the founders of Chirps Chips. Chirps are delicious tortilla chips made from crickets. Crickets, you say? Edible bugs? Definitely! Chirps is the food of the future.

"The first time I ate a bug was on a school field trip. And it was good. *Really* good. And that's when I had a light bulb moment. I wondered, if we eat shrimp and lobster, which are basically water bugs, why aren't we eating insects? Insects are packed with protein, vitamins, and minerals."

Jaye picked up from here. "People around the world have consumed bugs for thousands of years. Today, over two billion people enjoy bugs—from mealworm tacos to scorpion kebabs to fried grasshoppers. But for many people in America and Europe, there's still an 'ick factor' when it comes to bugs. I know, because I had it."

This was my cue to continue. "Chirps is changing that. We roast and grind our crickets into a powder to bake our chips. So there's nothing buggy that you can see or taste. We've sourced our crickets from a local farm, and they're fed the finest all-natural and organic ingredients. We feed them the good stuff so our customer gets the healthiest chip possible."

I hoped it was clear in my voice how intensely I believed in our product.

"Speaking of healthy." Jaye flashed graphs and charts she'd made onto the screen behind us. She talked about crickets using fewer resources, giving off less greenhouse gases, and providing more protein than cows and pigs. She explained how edible bugs could feed the world as the population continued to grow. In 2050, there will be nine billion people on the planet. What would they all eat?

Bugs were the answer.

As she spoke, I gazed into the audience. So many faces here for us, on our team. I shivered with excitement. We were smashing it.

And then I glimpsed Mrs. Montan waving her hand. My gaze followed hers to the side of the room. Spencer had just come in. He unzipped his jacket and leaned against the wall, listening to Jaye. He caught me staring, and sneered. I forced myself to look away.

My eyes shifted over to the judges. Mr. Reynolds pressed his fingertips together, his brow furrowed. Concentration? Disgust? I couldn't tell. Ms. Rees doodled on the notepad in front of her. Was she even listening to Jaye?

My chest tightened as an unexpected wave of fear crashed down around me. I dropped my head to catch my breath.

Jaye cleared her throat.

I snapped my head back up. How long had I been like

that? Five seconds? Five minutes? I wasn't sure.

It was my turn to speak.

To say something about crickets.

But I had absolutely no idea what came next.

CHAPTER 23
JAYE

Something was wrong with Hallie.

She hadn't picked up on my cue. Plastering a fake smile on my face, I shot her a sideways glance. I cleared my throat, forcing her to look up.

No, no, no . . .

All color had drained from her face. I tried to mentally will her into saying her lines, but she just stared into space.

Our plan was to go back and forth. She'd give facts, then I would.

I needed Hallie's crackling energy, her positive vibes. I couldn't do this without her. Chirps had been Hallie's idea—I was following her lead.

Should I ask the judges for a do-over? Walk off the stage?

I blinked rapidly, my gaze landing on Eddie. I remembered my dad telling him before his tournament that even if he couldn't hit a winner, he needed to return the ball. That there'd be other opportunities as long as he kept the ball in play.

I glanced at the clock. Only a few seconds had passed. I didn't think the judges had noticed Hallie's falter, but I couldn't let more time tick by. I began to speak.

"When people try our chips, they love them." I clicked on a photo of Owen greedily scooping nachos with his hands from the Ping-Pong table. I showed a photo of a blindfolded woman at the bake sale, comparing our chips with a popular no-bug brand. I described how in taste tests, our chips came out on top. I talked about our plans to grow the company.

I realized I now knew as much about edible bugs as Hallie did. Chirps was my company as much as hers.

"My grandma told us that in ancient China, a cricket on the hearth was considered good luck. A cricket on your plate will bring more than luck—nutrition, health, and an easy way to save the planet."

I checked the clock. Only five seconds left.

"Cricket chips are part of a new food category that's destined to become huge," Hallie suddenly spoke up, surprising me, back to her usual self. "Chirps is a tasty introduction to edible bugs, that's actually getting people to eat insects. Bug appétit!"

The audience clapped as Hallie and I squatted to grab the samples from the basket we'd brought onstage.

"You okay?" I whispered.

"Brain freeze." She looked embarrassed. "Thanks for saving it."

"That's what friends are for." I gave her hand a quick squeeze.

Haley exhaled. "Let's slay this."

She stood and spun around. "We've brought chips for you to try." She placed a bag in front of each judge, along with a tiny origami cricket.

"What's this?" Ms. Rees inspected it.

Haley explained how we'd infested the school and the town with colorful paper bugs to build excitement and advertise our ginormous nacho event.

"And you folded hundreds of these yourselves?" She sounded amazed.

I nodded. "But we had help. A lot of help."

"What kind of help?" Mr. Reynolds furrowed his eyebrows suspiciously.

"We made deals," I told him about our deal with Irv, with Dipti, and with Deanna and Bess.

Mr. Reynolds wanted to know about our pricing. I told him it cost $1.50 a bag to make and we were charging $3.00 a bag. He suggested we look for ways to bring the cost down.

"It's time for the moment of truth." Mr. Wuhan held up a chip and took a bite.

I held my breath as all the judges chewed and swallowed.

"It looks like a normal chip." Mr. Wuhan grinned. "And it tastes like a normal chip. Nicely seasoned, too."

Ms. Rees snapped her head in his direction. "Define normal, Caleb. A potato chip? A tortilla chip? These chips are in their own category. Unique." She looked at us. "I like that."

I thought Hallie might run across the stage and hug her.

"And I love all your innovative ideas. The origami. The

stickers. The cookbook recipe. The nachos." She beamed, clearly energized. "Is there anything you two didn't do?"

"Yes." I gulped. "We didn't sell two hundred bags of chips."

Hallie and I had decided to be up-front and honest, even though not completing the challenge would hurt us.

Mr. Reynolds tilted his head. "Why not?"

"We had cricket supply problems." Hallie detailed everything we'd been through.

The judges stopped smiling and scribbled notes. But I thought I saw Ms. Rees smirk when Hallie explained about her cricket hotel.

"Last question," Mr. Wuhan said. "If you won the money, how would you use it?"

"We planned to buy ready-made cricket powder to make things easier. But that may have to wait. We got a call this morning." Hallie paused for dramatic effect. "A natural food store wants to sell our chips!"

I jumped in. "We're using the money we made at the nacho event to pay Dipti back, so we need that winning money more than ever now. This way we can buy more crickets and better paper bags and actually sell our chips at a *real* store."

Mr. Wuhan told us we'd done a great job, and there was more applause. Suddenly Mr. Fletcher was back on stage, introducing the next startup.

Hallie and I were sent back to our seats.

All we could do now was wait.

CHAPTER 24
HALLIE

"What's for dinner?" I asked, entering Jaye's kitchen that night.

Jaye pointed to the steaming bowls of noodles and spiced fish. "Nai Nai made all my favorites."

"And those vegetable dumplings you like, Hallie." Nai Nai added from the stove. Her face was flushed from the sizzling heat of the pan. "Sit, sit."

A sixth chair had been pulled up to the table. This was the first time I was eating with Jaye's family, and I'd worn the multicolored crocheted dress I found last week at a vintage store. It was the happiest dress I owned.

"First, take a photo." Mr. Wu positioned me and Jaye then raised the camera. "Show me your winning smiles."

But I hadn't stopped smiling since this afternoon when Mr. Fletcher had announced that Chirps had won!

Jaye and I were both stunned when he called our names. It turns out the judges loved our mission, how we were trying to change the way people ate with our chips. They said the innovative ways we brought attention to the chips and the deals we made is what put us above all the other teams.

Mrs. Wu placed the check and the tickets to New York City in the center of the table.

We were moving on to the State Pitch Competition in New York City! Posie and her partner had come in second place and were going with us. It still felt unreal.

"You deserved to win," Jaye's dad said while we ate.

"You showed excellent business sense. You know, the whole time I was thinking: why two hundred bags? It's a random number. It means nothing more than one hundred and fifty bags."

"Actually, we sold one hundred and sixty-three," Jaye corrected him.

"Jaye's good at keeping track of things like that," I bragged for her. "She did all the deals."

I filled them in on everything Jaye hadn't shared. I even told them how the kids at Pitch Club are always asking for Jaye's opinion.

"You've found another talent, Jaye." Mrs. Wu motioned to the check and the tickets displayed in the place of honor on the table. "Business."

"And art," Eddie piped up. "She's good at origami."

"And soccer. I saw her play. And cello, right?" I gave her a friendly nudge. "She has lots of talents."

The tops of Jaye's cheeks grew pink. She looked

embarrassed, but I could tell she was proud.

You see, we had it. *The Connection.* Me and Jaye.

I realized it onstage when I'd gotten so nervous and almost blew it for us. Jaye had sensed I was spiraling. She *knew* without us talking or anything. And the way she'd jumped in and said my lines, no one would've guessed that she wasn't supposed to be speaking.

As Nai Nai leaned over to refill my plate for a second time, her parents wanted to know our plans for the next competition.

We had none. Yet.

"We'll figure it out, right?" I said to Jaye.

Then I heard the repetitive thump of a ball bouncing. I looked out the window. Spencer was shooting hoops in his driveway.

Jaye didn't even glance that way.

"Hallie, tell them about the hotel."

"I heard you say this to the judges." Mrs. Wu folded her napkin and leaned forward.

"She had room service!" Eddie cried.

"Her mom thought there was a ghost," Jaye put in.

"But then the exterminator came," Eddie added.

I told the story, and the laughter of Jaye and her family made all the sounds of Spencer fade away.

After we'd helped with the dishes, my mom texted from out front. I slipped on my parka and handed Jaye a box I'd wrapped in shiny purple paper.

"What's this?" She scrunched her face.

"A surprise. Don't open it 'til I'm back home and on the phone with you. Promise?"

"Weird," Jaye said, but she promised.

An hour later, wearing my polka-dot flannel pajamas and sitting cross-legged on my bed, I video-called her. "Do you have the box?"

Jaye held it up. She wore an oversize pink sleep shirt. "Can I open it now?"

"Go for it."

She tore off the wrapping paper and lifted the lid. "A bottle of neon-green nail polish. Colored string. Gummi worms. A watermelon face mask sheet." She shot me a quizzical look. "I'm not getting it."

"Sleepover in a box! We're having a virtual sleepover." I panned to my bedspread, showing the same bottle of nail polish, the friendship bracelet string, gummi worms, and face mask. "And we can watch the same movie at the same time. I'm thinking something set in New York City."

"I can't believe you did this!" Jaye tore open the bag of gummi worms. "You're the best!"

"You're *nacho*-bad yourself." I grinned.

Jaye didn't miss a beat. "Our friend-*chip* rules!"

EAT BUGS WAS INSPIRED BY A TRUE STORY.

Laura D'Asaro and Rose Wang, cofounders of the *real* Chirps, were roommates at Harvard University. While studying one summer in Tanzania, Laura (an off-and-on vegetarian) walked by a street vendor selling fried caterpillars. Wanting to do as the locals do, she tried one and thought it tasted like lobster. Meanwhile, half a world away in China, Rose was dared to eat a fried scorpion, and she thought it tasted like shrimp. When Laura and Rose got back to school, they started researching why people ate bugs in other parts of the world and not in America with a plan to form a company. They were joined by another student, Meryl Breidbart, and the trio experimented with insect-inspired foods. They tried everything from mealworm tacos to cricket sushi before landing on cricket powder, which they used to make America's favorite snack—chips! They entered pitch contests and eventually won enough money to fund their startup. But few people believed their insect-protein chips would be a success. Laura and Rose had to call four hundred tortilla-chip manufacturers before one was willing to make their chips. Laura and Rose appeared on *Shark Tank* and landed a deal with Mark Cuban. After a lot of hard work, their chips are now sold on thousands of store shelves across the nation, and their company has helped educate millions of people on how food impacts climate change.

You can learn more about their company at eatchirps.com.

HALLIE AND JAYE'S EASY NACHOS

(THE REGULAR-SIZE VERSION—NOT WORLD-RECORD SIZE)

** Always ask an adult for help with
preheating the oven and with placing
the pans in and taking them out of the oven.

INGREDIENTS

- tortilla chips—or use our cricket chips!

- 1 cup salsa (mild for Hallie, spicy for Jaye,

you choose your fave)

- 1 can of black or refried beans, drained

(or don't use beans—your call)

- 2 cups shredded cheese

(we like the Mexican blend best)

DIRECTIONS

1. Preheat the oven to 350°F (180°C).

(Always have an adult help you with the oven.)

2. Line a baking pan with foil, then spray with

cooking spray (so your nachos won't stick).

3. Spread the chips in a thin layer over the whole pan

(we use one or two LARGE handfuls per person).

4. Spread the salsa and beans on top and sprinkle the

cheese on last.

5. Bake for 10 minutes, or until the cheese melts.

6. Serve with a side of sour cream or guacamole.

7. Yum! Bug appétit!

HEATHER TALKS WITH LAURA AND ROSE

Heather: Hi, Laura and Rose! I'm excited to chat about the "real" Chirps with you. As you know, I reimagined your story and set it in middle school instead of college, but I wanted to make sure to incorporate a lot of events that actually happened.

Laura: You definitely did!

Heather: In the book, Irv doesn't believe in Hallie and Jaye's business at first. Other people also doubt their vision. In real life, did you experience the same thing?

Rose: All the time. People were always telling us no. When we went out to look for people to help us with the costs of starting a business (money to buy ingredients, etc.), we gave our pitch to a well-known investor and when we were done, he turned to us and said, "I've been an investor for ten years, and this is the *worst* idea I ever heard."

Heather: That's horrible. How did you react?

Laura: We thought he was wrong. We were completely convinced Chirps would work. However, it did make us realize we needed proof to convince other investors why it was a good idea. After that, we launched a Kickstarter campaign, which is an online fundraising platform. We got 1,295 orders and raised $70,000 in just one month! And that proved that people wanted our product.

Rose: But then we had to make the cricket chips, and we had a really hard time finding a place to do that. We called four hundred food manufacturers, and every single one of them said no.

Heather: Did you ever think about quitting?

Laura: No, we were very stubborn. Also, we had all the Kickstarter customers waiting for their Chirps. We had to deliver the product.

Rose: I was much more the pessimist. I remember getting sad and thinking, "This is never going to happen." But I had a lot to prove. After college, I had turned down a really good job offer from Microsoft to build our startup. My parents and friends thought I'd made a huge mistake, but I believed in Chirps and what Laura and I were building.

Laura: So for three months, we kept calling and calling manufacturers. It was scary to talk to people we didn't know and try to sell them on what we were doing . . . especially telling them about our secret ingredient—crickets!

Rose: *Finally* we found one manufacturer willing to help us. Tammy liked that we were doing something different. She seemed much more open to listening and hearing us compared to the other people we talked to. You need to totally believe in what you're doing, because 99 percent of the people will be quick to tell you all the ways it won't work.

Heather: Another real event that appears in the book is the giant nachos. I love that you set the world's record (on RecordSetter) in 2017 for the largest serving of nachos. It was seventy feet long and weighed 5,022 pounds—wow!

Laura: Here's what happened . . . we'd gotten a huge order from a national summer camp for 10,000 pounds of our cricket chips. We had all those chips ready and packaged in big ten-pound bags, but then the camp decided to buy only 8,000 pounds, and we were left with 2,000 pounds of chips. We had to figure out what to do with them, because we couldn't sell them to stores in those huge bags.

Rose: Earth Day was coming up, so we decided that throwing a giant nacho party in San Francisco would be a great way to get a lot of people interested in eating bugs.

Laura: I had broken world records before,* so that's how I got the idea. It's a great way to capture people's attention.

Rose: Over one thousand people showed up. We got a lot of media coverage, which gave our brand some good exposure. Plus, the event was sustainable through and through, which was one of our goals! We didn't want to spend any money, so we asked thirty of our friends to volunteer to help. And then we donated the leftover nachos—and there was *a lot!*— to San Francisco homeless shelters.

Heather: In the book, during the pitch competition, Hallie forgets her lines. You've done tons of pitches, and even appeared on *Shark Tank*, have you ever messed up?

Laura: Definitely, oh my, there are so many stories! What happened to Hallie happened to me exactly. I forgot my pitch midway, and Rose, without skipping a beat, just picked it up. And we won that one!

Heather: What caused you to forget?

Laura: Pitching is scary. It's not something I was comfortable doing. Rose and I had this ongoing argument because I liked to memorize every single line word-for-word . . .

Rose: And I like to memorize just the concepts and major points. This way if you fumble or freeze, you don't get as rattled.

Laura: We got a lot better at pitching.

Rose: Yeah, we can pitch almost anything now. But we practiced a ton. Before one competition, we practiced together for twelve hours nonstop.

Heather: What was it like to build a business with a friend?

Rose: Building a business is tough. It takes a lot of hard work and long hours. It can test your friendship like nothing else, but I think partnering with your friend makes it more fun and seem more real. Laura "gets" me more than anyone, because we did this together.

Laura: Rose pushed me to do things I didn't think I could do, like pitch in front of hundreds of people. We had a special kind of magic together. It was always us against the world.

© Ben Von Wong

*Laura currently holds the world record for the fastest time to crawl a mile and was part of the team that built the largest cardboard box fort.

HEATHER ALEXANDER is the author of numerous fiction and nonfiction books for kids, including the Wallace and Grace series, The Amazing Stardust Friends series, and A Child's Introduction to . . . series. In addition to writing books, she also works as a children's book editor. She grew up in New Jersey and now lives in Los Angeles, California, with her family and beagle, Luna. Since meeting Rose and Laura, she can't stop munching on cricket chips while writing (cheddar is her favorite flavor).

Visit her at heatheralexanderbooks.com.